Gabe put his arms around Cara and pulled her into a gentle hug.

"If the answer's here, we'll find it."

She had gone very still in his embrace, but when he spoke she relaxed, leaned against him, into him, taking the comfort he offered. The shared contact, the warmth, eased the old pain even more, and he wondered that he hadn't realized it would do that.

"Thank you," he said, lifting her chin up with a gentle finger. "For still caring so much after all this time."

He didn't even realize what he was doing until his lips brushed hers. It hadn't been a conscious decision. But she was there, so close, looking up at him with that unwavering steadiness.

And the next thing he knew, he'd done it. He'd kissed her.

He couldn't regret it. But the acknowledgment didn't tell him how to deal with the unwelcome fact that Cara Thorpe had somehow stirred his first real interest in a woman in longer than he cared to remember.

Dear Reader,

Let's extend our summer lovin' with this month's Silhouette Romantic Suspense offerings. Reader-favorite Kathleen Creighton will enthrall you with *Daredevil's Run* (#1523), the latest in her miniseries THE TAKEN. Here, an embittered man reunites with his long-lost love as they go on a death-defying adventure in the wilderness. You'll feel the heat from Cindy Dees's *Killer Affair* (#1524), the third book in SEDUCTION SUMMER. In this series, a serial killer murders amorous couples on the beach, and no lover is safe. Don't miss the exciting conclusion to this sizzling roller-coaster ride!

When a handsome hero receives a mysterious postcard, he joins forces to find its sender with the woman who secretly loves him. Can they overcome a shared tragedy and face the future together? Find out in Justine Davis's emotional tale *Her Best Friend's Husband* (#1525), which is part of her popular REDSTONE, INCORPORATED miniseries. Finally, let's give a big welcome to Jennifer Morey, who debuts in the line with *The Secret Soldier* (#1526), and begins her miniseries ALL McQUEEN'S MEN. In this action-packed story, a dangerous—and ultrasexy—military man must rescue a kidnapped scientist. As they risk life and limb, they discover an unforgettable chemistry.

This month, you'll find love against the odds and adventures lurking around every corner. Enjoy these gems from Silhouette Romantic Suspense!

Sincerely,

Patience Smith
Senior Editor

Her Best
FRIEND'S HUSBAND

Justine Davis

Silhouette®

Romantic

SUSPENSE

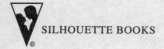

SILHOUETTE BOOKS

ISBN-13: 978-0-373-27595-3
ISBN-10:   0-373-27595-1

HER BEST FRIEND'S HUSBAND

Copyright © 2008 by Janice Davis Smith

Visit Silhouette Books at www.eHarlequin.com

Printed in U.S.A.

Selected Books by Justine Davis

Silhouette Romantic Suspense

One Last Chance #517
Wicked Secrets #555
Left at the Altar #596
Out of the Dark #638
The Morning Side of Dawn #674
†*Lover Under Cover* #698
†*Leader of the Pack* #728
†*A Man To Trust* #805
†*Gage Butler's Reckoning* #841
†*Badge of Honor* #871
†*Clay Yeager's Redemption* #926
The Return of Luke McGuire #1036
Just Another Day in Paradise #1141
The Prince's Wedding #1190
One of These Nights #1201
In His Sights #1318
Second-Chance Hero #1351
Dark Reunion #1452
Deadly Temptation #1493
Her Best Friend's Husband #1525

†Trinity Street West
*Redstone, Incorporated

JUSTINE DAVIS

lives on Puget Sound in Washington. Her interests outside of writing are sailing, doing needlework, horseback riding and driving her restored 1967 Corvette roadster—top down, of course.

Justine says that years ago, during her career in law enforcement, a young man she worked with encouraged her to try for a promotion to a position that was, at the time, occupied only by men. "I succeeded, became wrapped up in my new job, and that man moved away, never, I thought, to be heard from again. Ten years later he appeared out of the woods of Washington State, saying he'd never forgotten me and would I please marry him. With that history, how could I write anything but romance?"

Chapter 1

"It's time, Gabe."

Gabriel Taggert looked at his father-in-law and wanted to punch him out. Which was odd, because he admired, respected, and yes, loved the man. And he would never do it, since at his own six-foot-one he towered over the slighter man.

"He's right, dear," Gwen Waldron said quietly, agreeing with her husband. She usually did. Not that she wasn't more than capable of standing up for herself if she truly disagreed; it was just that the forty-years'-married couple rarely differed in opinion.

"Just like that?"

Gabe's voice came out low and harsh, which startled him. Shouldn't he be over it by now? They all—meaning every well-intentioned person who knew what had happened—told him it was a process that was individual, that everyone had to do it at their own pace and in their own way. But despite the platitude, he was fairly certain most of them would expect his world to have gone on by now.

"Do you think we like this any more than you do?"

For the first time the undertone of emotion broke through in Earl Waldron's voice. Somehow that made the tightness in Gabe's gut ease a little.

"But it's been eight years." Gwen put her hand on his arm then, a touch he treasured because of who she was and hated because of who she wasn't. "You know she'd have been in touch, no matter what happened, if she could."

He supposed the worst part of what he was feeling was the knowledge, somewhere buried deep, that they were right. He fought to keep it buried, but with both of them digging at it now, he wasn't sure he could. The simple fact was, his wife was gone, vanished so completely that not having found a body didn't make it any less likely she was dead.

"We're not asking for a decision here and now. Just promise you'll consider it," Earl said. "Really consider it, son. We need to move on. And so do you."

"All right." He owed them that much, and he couldn't help it if the words came out a little sharp.

He stood there on the deck of the hundred-and-forty-nine foot boat that was his world these days and watched them walk down the gangplank. They'd been a huge part of his life for so long—accepting him as the son they'd never had and still treating him that way, even though the link between them was gone— that he couldn't imagine going on without them.

But then, he'd gone on with an even bigger piece missing. Not well, or with any particular grace, but he had gone on.

"Everything all right?"

The soft inquiry came from behind him, and Gabe turned to look at his friend and boss, Joshua Redstone, who was also the designer and builder of this dream ship. Gabe had been in the depths of the darkest hole when Josh had offered him the job of heading up his boat-building enterprise. And when the desk-oriented job had begun to pall a couple of years ago, Josh had seemed to sense it. He'd given Gabe the chance to be at sea again, with the captaincy of this lovely vessel, the latest and biggest to bear the Redstone name.

It was to be, Josh had told him, the literal flagship of Redstone, not to be sold as others had been, but to be kept for the use of the Redstone family. From division managers to file clerks, anybody who worked for Redstone, Incorporated and had the need would have access to the boat.

And Gabe had been among the first to learn exactly what Josh meant; the first weeklong cruise he'd captained had been for the concierge of one of the Redstone Resorts, whose husband had died in a traffic accident. She was but one of thousands of employees, and at a relatively low level on the Redstone chain, but Josh, as he always did, had heard about the death and had offered the boat to the entire family.

"Gabe?"

He snapped out of the memory as Josh gently prodded. "I...I'm not sure."

"Were they your in-laws?" Josh's drawl was barely discernable, telling Gabe how carefully he was picking his words. "Hope's parents?"

"Yes."

"Tough," Josh said.

Gabe turned to look at his boss then. "Yes," he agreed.

"They made a special trip out here to see you?"

Gabe nodded. And then, because no one knew better exactly how he felt, he let it out.

"They want my wife declared dead."

Josh was silent for a long moment. If it had been anyone else, Gabe might have assumed he had nothing to say, but the head of Redstone, Inc., was never one to speak lightly or without thought. That characteristic delay—and the drawl—gave some, to their detriment, the idea he was slow or lazy. They inevitably spent time afterward musing on the cost of their assumptions.

"They want their daughter declared dead?" Josh finally said, quietly.

And there, with the insight typical of him, Josh reminded him gently that their loss was as great as his. Greater, perhaps; they'd had Hope Waldron for twenty-nine years, he for only six of those.

"I know, I know." Gabe shoved a hand through his dark hair, realizing only after he'd done it that he'd still, after all this time, raised both hands as if he were wearing his officer's combination cap, to be removed before the gesture and resettled after precisely an inch and a half above his eyebrows, according to navy regs.

"Old habits die hard," Josh observed mildly, and Gabe knew he'd caught the lapse. "Old thoughts sometimes die harder."

"How long did it take you?"

The question escaped him before he could block it. Not for anything, even to ease his own pain, would he intentionally call up bad memories for this man he admired, respected, even loved, as did most who worked for him. Josh Redstone had built an empire that spanned the globe, employed thousands, and Gabe would be willing to bet there wasn't one of them who wouldn't walk into hell for the man. In part because they knew he'd do it for them—and had.

"I'm sorry," Gabe began, but Josh waved him to silence.

"How long did it take me to accept that she was gone?" Josh asked. "In my head, I knew it right away. But then, she died in my arms. I felt her go."

Gabe's breath caught. He hadn't known that. He'd known Elizabeth Redstone had died of cancer several years ago, known that Josh had been alone ever since, knew the common wisdom at Redstone was that she'd been his soul mate and he would never even try to replace her. But Gabe had never really thought about the details of it. Hope, he thought, would likely have had the whole story within minutes of meeting the man; she had always been good at getting people to open up.

An odd smile curved Josh's mouth, lifting it at one corner in an expression of ironic sadness. "I never thought of that as a particular advantage before, other than being with her until the end. But from your view, it is, isn't it? At least I knew, without doubt."

Gabe couldn't deny that, and instead fastened on Josh's answer to his question. He repeated his boss's words back. "You said you knew it in your head."

Josh's mouth quirked, and the steady gray eyes closed for a moment. Then he opened them and looked at Gabe. "You always were detail oriented."

"Comes from years of dealing with politically oriented navy brass," Gabe answered. "Most of the time what they didn't say was more important than what they did."

"I'm sure," Josh agreed. And then, after a moment, answered what Gabe hadn't really asked. "I'm not sure my heart, my gut, have accepted it yet. I know, logically, that it's crazy after all these years, but I still catch myself expecting to hear her voice, or thinking that she's just in the next room...."

Gabe smothered a sigh. That was not what he'd wanted to hear. He'd wanted to hear that it was over, sealed away in some silent, impenetrable place in Josh's mind, never bothering him, never surfacing unless he wanted it to. If Joshua Redstone, one of the strongest—and strongest-minded—men he'd ever met, couldn't get past this, what hope did he have?

"What brought this on now, after all this time?" Josh asked.

"The U.S. Postal Service," Gabe said wryly.

Josh blinked. "The Postal Service?"

"They just delivered a postcard to Hope's best friend. From Hope, mailed right before she disappeared. It really upset them."

Josh let out a low whistle. "Ouch. Eight years?"

To his own surprise, Gabe had to stifle a chuckle. Josh, he knew, would never tolerate that kind of thing. Redstone wasn't consistently in the top five highest-rated places to work because it was easy. It was Josh himself, and his reputation, that made a Redstone job among the most coveted. He hired the best, let them do what they did best, paid them well, treated them all with fairness, and mostly stayed out of their way. But above all he let them know that if they needed it, the full power of the Redstone empire was behind them.

"Why don't you head for open water?" Josh said.

Gabe drew back slightly. "What?"

Josh shrugged. "Take her out. Clear your head."

Only Josh Redstone would make an offer like that, to take a hundred-and-forty-nine-foot luxury yacht, complete with a media room and helipad, out for a spin as if it were a new car rather than the latest, and as yet unnamed, design from his fertile and incredible mind.

"Thank you," Gabe said automatically, "but—"

"You saying you don't do your best thinking at sea?"

Gabe's mouth quirked. "You can take the boy out of the navy, but you can't take the navy out of the boy?"

Josh grinned. "Something like that."

Neither of them mentioned that in Gabe's case, he hadn't been taken out of the navy, he'd quit. Gabe knew he'd had no choice, and Josh, when he'd learned the full story of what had driven a man who'd once chosen the navy as his career to leave, had answered in the best possible way: he'd offered Gabe a way out that didn't require him to leave his love of ships and the water behind.

"I've got to head back to my office," Josh said, and Gabe knew the reluctance he heard in his boss's voice was real. Josh was not an office-bound executive, even at Redstone Headquarters, which was as much a paragon of comfort and thoughtful design as this boat was.

"Take her out," he said again. "Put all this on the back burner, focus on something else for a while. It'll help you work through it, where chewing on it up front won't."

Gabe smiled at the rustic simile, thinking again of those who made the mistake of assuming the drawl and the down-home manner were all there was to Josh. It amazed him how anyone could look at the size and scope of Redstone and think that anyone less than a genius could have built it, but people were often ruled by their own filters and perceptions, a fact Josh frequently used to his advantage. And since his naval career had come to a crashing end because of such people, Gabe couldn't help but appreciate Josh's talent in that area.

"And," Josh added as he went down the gangway steps, "if you need anything, if Redstone can help, call."

Gabe nodded, knowing that what would have been a casual offer, never really intended for acceptance from most people, was something quite different coming from Josh Redstone. When he offered help to one of his huge family—which meant anyone who worked for and with him—he meant it.

In the seven years he'd worked for Josh, overseeing the smallest but one of the most loved—by Josh, anyway—divisions of the empire, so small it didn't even have its own name but rather existed as a sideline of the aviation division, he'd both seen and heard of the kinds of things Redstone had done for its people. The cruise he'd captained for the bereaved family had only been the latest in a very long string of things done that Josh took for granted; if you were Redstone, Redstone helped when you needed it.

Later that morning, when Gabe stood out on deck, having let the eager young first mate take the wheel for a while—although the boat had the newer, joystick type of controls, Josh was enough of a traditionalist to have also included the wheel—he had to admit his boss was right. Being out here, on blue water with the smell of the salt air and the sounds of the sleek red-and-gray vessel cutting powerfully through the water, soothed his mind and soul in a way nothing else could.

By the time they were back at the dock and he was overseeing the cleanup and making his log entry, he was resigned. He would do as the Waldrons had asked; he wouldn't fight them. Gwen's pain had been too real, too palpable, and he couldn't stand in the way of anything that might ease it, no matter how ambivalent he might be about it.

Besides, he thought, it might be a relief to him as well, when people asked, to be able to say with some truth that she was dead. It was so much more finite than "She vanished," less painful than

"She walked out on me without a word," and certainly less uncomfortable than "I have no idea where my wife is."

Of course, even if Hope were declared legally dead, it wouldn't resolve anything for him. He knew too well that it would always be there, hovering, that her "death" would be of legal status only, that he would be forever no closer to knowing what had really happened. No closer to knowing if she'd had an accident, or if the worse-case scenario that haunted him was true, that she'd been murdered and dumped somewhere.

But after eight years, he'd gotten better at living with that. He'd learned—

"Captain?"

He looked up from the ship's log entry at Mark Spencer, the young first mate he'd given the wheel to earlier.

"I thought you'd gone for lunch."

"I was, but…there's someone here to see you, sir," Mark said, seeming oddly nervous.

"The Waldrons?" he asked, hoping they would understand why he'd disappeared out to sea after they'd left.

"No. A…woman."

The way he said it, as if he'd had to choose among many descriptions, alerted Gabe. Whoever it was, she'd made an impression. Hiding the first real smile he'd felt coming on since his in-laws had arrived this morning, he stood up.

"She asked for you personally, by name," Mark added, unable to mask the curiosity in his eyes. Gabe read the speculation there, knew what the younger man was wondering; had their reclusive, loner captain been holding out on them?

Not likely, he muttered inwardly, and the smile that threatened this time was wryly self-knowing.

"She give you a name, Mark?"

"Cara. She said you'd know."

Any urge at all to smile vanished. It seemed his painful day wasn't over yet.

"Where did you put her?"

"The main salon."

"Go see if she needs anything, a drink, food," he ordered, wanting a moment alone to deal with this next surprise.

"Already done, sir." Mark's formal tone told him his voice had been a bit sharp.

"Good job," he said, careful to keep his own tone even this time.

"I'm Redstone," Mark said simply.

That got him the smile, and it was genuine. "Thanks, Mark. Please tell her I'll be there in a moment."

"Yes, sir."

The young man executed a turn snappy enough to earn him approval from any Naval officer, and left the bridge.

Cara.

Gabe sank back into the raised captain's chair for a moment. She'd have that postcard with her, he thought. She'd expect him to look at it, read it. And for a moment he wondered if he could do this, if he could rip open those old wounds once more. If he could survive it if he did.

And then he realized it didn't matter. The wounds had never healed; the constant dig of uncertainty had kept them open and bleeding beneath the surface. There might be scars over them, but it wouldn't take much to tear those scars away.

A postcard would do it.

Chapter 2

*C*ara *Thorpe,* Gabe thought as he quickly finished his short log entry on the day's cruise.

She'd not only been Hope's best friend since elementary school, they'd been like sisters, and all the time he and Hope had been together, she'd been on the periphery, somewhere. She'd been so quiet she seemed to fade into the background, so much so that Gabe hadn't minded much when Hope had insisted she go with them to some party, or attend a function with other people. He'd even tried to set her up with one of his buddies now and then, someone he thought might see past the quiet exterior, but something always seemed to get in the way of it actually happening.

Cara had always been bright, beneath the shyness, and she'd gone away to get her master's degree shortly before he and Hope had married. She'd been home for the wedding, but Gabe hadn't seen her again until after Hope had vanished. Gwen had called her then, of course, to see if she had any idea where Hope was, or if she'd heard from her. She had, in fact, had a phone message from Hope that last morning, but it wasn't much help, only an excited promise to call her back with big news, the biggest.

The call had never come.

Cara had immediately come home to help in the search. Gabe only vaguely remembered the quiet, withdrawn young woman's departure several weeks later; he'd been too sunk in his own misery to worry overmuch about hers.

As he rose once more and headed for the large main salon of the boat, he shouldn't have been surprised that she'd show up now, not after being the one to receive that much-belated postcard.

Cara had likely never given up on the possibility of finding Hope alive and well. Hope had always said Cara was the most staunchly loyal person she'd ever known. That she'd often said it while pointing out how in her view that accolade didn't apply to him was something he tried not to dwell on. Hope's interpretation of loyalty hadn't quite meshed with his, and certainly not with the navy's. Which was one of the reasons, although not the main one, that he was no longer in the uniform he'd once expected to wear for life.

He slid open the large, glass door to the salon. It moved with the well-balanced, smooth silence expected on any Redstone vessel, and the woman seated with her back to him on the deeply cushioned couch upholstered in a rich, slate-gray fabric that looked like suede, didn't turn. For a moment he stood there, staring at the back of her head as sunlight streamed in through the glass.

Had her hair always been that rich, autumn-leaves color? He remembered it as just sort of brown. Long and straight, and plain. Maybe it was the sunlight, although he'd certainly seen her in the sun before. If she'd done something more than just cut it so that it fell in soft waves just to her shoulders, it was subtle, yet made a world of difference.

And then, as if she'd sensed his presence, she stood up, turned.

And stunned him.

The quiet little mouse was gone. This was the woman who'd left Mark speechless. This was a tall, perfectly curved, vibrant, auburn-haired woman dressed in a cool, pale green that reminded him of mint ice cream. It was luscious on a hot, Southern California day.

This was a woman who looked back at him confidently with bright blue eyes that had so often avoided his before. A woman who walked toward him with an easy grace quite unlike the awkwardly tall, quiet mouse, who had always seemed to be hesitant or hasty, depending on the circumstances.

"Gabe," she said softly as she came to a halt before him.

Had her voice always been so low and husky? Did he even know, could he even remember? She had always been so quiet, at least around him; Hope had said she talked all the time when they were alone, so he'd assumed it was just him she wasn't comfortable around. He'd even asked her once, on one of those days so long ago, why she didn't like him. She'd blushed furiously, said she liked him fine.

"Cara," he said finally. "You've…changed."

"Well, I should hope so," she said with amusement. "In eight years. You, on the other hand, naval officer or not, are still tall, dark and ramrod-straight Gabriel Taggert, aren't you?"

He didn't smile; Hope had teased him far too much about the military carriage that had been drilled into him early on for him to take the echoed comment lightly. More than once he'd been driven beyond irritation by her insistence that he learn how to "unbend," as if the way he stood or carried himself meant he was rigid and inflexible in mind as well.

"I'm sorry," she said after a moment of silence. "I didn't mean that in a bad way."

He shrugged one shoulder. "You're just repeating what she always said."

"I know." Something came into her voice then, a sort of regret. "I shouldn't have said it. It took me a long time to realize she was really digging at you."

His mouth quirked then. "Me, too."

"I thought she was proud." Those blue eyes, that he somehow hadn't remembered as quite so vivid, lowered then, in a momentary reversion to the mouse of old. "I would have been," she added softly.

The simple admission startled him, and to his surprise, moved him. "Thank you," he said, not sure what else to say. This woman had been part of a life he'd lost long ago, yet she looked and seemed so different now that he wasn't sure what to think of her at all.

She moved then, reaching for the small shoulder bag that matched the light green of her silky shirt. A gold chain glinted at the neckline, vanishing behind the first button. He wondered idly where it ended up, and sucked in a shocked breath as an image shot through his mind of some personal locket or charm resting gently atop breasts that were all woman.

He quashed the image instantly, feeling a bit as if he'd had a lustful thought about the proverbial girl next door. But he couldn't deny the fact Cara Thorpe had filled out some. Nicely.

She removed something from a side pocket of the purse and held it out to him, thankfully unaware of the misfire of his imagination.

"Obviously, this is why I'm here."

It was the postcard, he realized. And caught himself looking at it much as if it were a venomous snake he'd stumbled onto.

He couldn't face it, not yet. So he looked at her hands instead. Long, slim fingers, neat, not-too-long nails finished with a subtle shine that spoke of care but not vanity. No ring, he noted, glancing at her left hand. Nor any sign of one that had been worn for any length of time.

She was exactly one month younger than Hope, he remembered; the two women had celebrated together at the halfway point between their birthdays every year. So she was thirty-seven now. He found it hard to believe, if she'd left mousehood behind very long ago, that she hadn't been snapped up by some man. He couldn't be the only one who'd noticed the curves. And the eyes. And the new, confident air.

"Maybe I shouldn't have come here, but I thought you'd want to…see it."

He realized at her quiet words that he'd left her standing there with that damned thing in her hand for too long. He shifted his gaze to the card. The sight of Hope's familiar scrawl, as unruly as she had sometimes been, sent a jab of the old ache through him.

With the sense that he was breaching a dam holding back a host of pain, a dam it had taken him years to build, he reached out and took it.

She'd managed it, Cara thought. He'd taken the card from her, and she'd managed to keep from touching him in the process. That was success, progress even, wasn't it?

And for the moment, he was staring at the postcard in his hand, focused on it with that quiet intensity she'd never forgotten. She could look at him now, couldn't she? He'd never realize, or if he did, he'd think she was just watching for his reaction.

As, indeed, she would be.

Among other things.

Because now that she was face-to-face with him again, even after all this time, there was no denying that watching Gabriel Taggert do anything was and had always been one of her favorite activities.

She wanted to laugh at herself, as she had for so many years. She'd put girlish memories away, shaking her head in wry amusement whenever she thought of him and her own silly fantasies. But what she'd been able to do before, when she'd thought she'd never see him again, seemed impossible now that he was standing in front of her, all the six-plus feet, lean muscles, near-black hair and light-hazel eyes of him.

But she had laughed, back then. What else could you do when you realized you were a walking, breathing cliché? The only thing she hadn't been sure of was which cliché was the worst, falling for a man in uniform…or falling for her best friend's husband.

Not that she'd ever done anything about it. It wasn't in her. For the most part she played by the rules, and always had. She'd gotten more adventurous as she'd gotten older—oddly, her daring streak had begun about the time Hope disappeared—but the basic code never faltered: there were just some things you didn't do.

She'd known instinctively that it wasn't in Gabe, either, to betray his wife or his vows. Not that he ever would have for her, anyway, even if he had been that kind of man. Not for the quiet, withdrawn little girl she'd been; no man would have cheated with the likes of her.

But even if she'd been some gorgeous, chic, supermodel type, Gabe just wasn't that kind of man. Which, she knew, had been a big part of the attraction for her in the first place.

The problem now was, all the things she'd consoled herself with for the last eight years had been blown to bits.

It was a stupid kid thing, she'd told herself repeatedly. *You just wanted what you didn't have. It wasn't Gabe, not really. You just wanted what Hope had, not the exact person Hope had.*

She'd told herself that again and again, until she'd almost sold herself on the idea.

Until now.

Uh-oh, she muttered inwardly. She hadn't seen Gabe Taggert in years, and yet within five minutes the old feelings were as strong as ever.

At least he doesn't know, she told herself. She was spared that humiliation. She'd done that, at least, kept her silly feelings hidden from the man she could never have.

And you'll keep it that way, she ordered herself sternly. *Hope is still here, between us, and she always will be.*

She made herself focus on the present, watching as Gabe's face, tanned and attractively weathered from years on the water, changed as he looked at the postcard. The shock she had expected; it mirrored her own reaction. The envelope it had come in hadn't given a clue to the jolt that awaited, and the letter of apology from the U.S. Postal Service had been wryly amusing. But then she'd turned over the colorful mountain scene, wondering who had taken some long-ago vacation she was only now learning about, to see the handwriting that had once been nearly as familiar as her own. The energetic and wild scrawl had made her heart leap before she even realized why, before she saw the postmark and her mind jumped in with the explanation.

"That looks like Hope's writing," she'd said aloud at the time.

And then, seeing the signature crammed tightly in on the side edge of the card full of bursts of words that read like Hope's chatter, realizing it *was* Hope's handwriting, had made the bottom drop out of her world.

Thanks to Hope's parents Gabe had known this was coming, had known what she was handing him, but his shock seemed no less great; she understood that seeing it was different than simply knowing it existed. It was the difference between knowing something in your head and in your heart.

"Two miracles in one week," he muttered, and Cara knew exactly what he was reading, the last lines of scribbling that wrapped around the rest in typical Hope fashion; planning her writing space ahead had never been her style. The excess of exclamation points had.

Two miracles in one week, Cara!! I can't wait to tell you! I will as soon as I can, I promise. I would now, if Gabe were only here instead of out on that damned boat.

She remembered those words as clearly as if she were reading them again now.

He lifted his gaze to her face then. Those gold-flecked hazel eyes focused on her and she fought down the instinctive leap of her pulse.

"Do you have any idea what she was talking about?"

Cara shook her head. "All I know is how excited she sounded in that phone message, the day before she…disappeared."

He looked at the card again. Read the words again, and then again. Cara tried to imagine what it must feel like for him, to see this message from the woman he'd loved, to hold something she'd touched, after all this time.

"I'm sorry about the jab," she said. "About you being gone, I mean."

Gabe looked up at her, gave a one-shouldered shrug. "It doesn't matter. I know how she felt. I got used to it."

"I never understood that," Cara said softly. "She knew what your career was, and yet…."

Gabe's mouth quirked. "She wouldn't be the first woman to fall for a uniform, and then find the reality of military life too much to handle."

"But she loved you, not the uniform," Cara exclaimed.

"Maybe," Gabe said.

There hadn't been a trace of self-pity or bitterness in his voice, only the lingering uncertainty of a man who had pondered the question for a very long time.

Cara couldn't imagine what that was like, either, to have to wonder if the person you loved really loved you back, or just an idea you represented. She wanted to hug him, but knew quite well he wouldn't welcome the gesture.

And knew even better that it would be the worst thing she could possibly do for her own equilibrium. Just standing here with him was taking a toll on her stability.

He looked back at the postcard once more. Turned it over, stared at the picture for a moment, then flipped back to the side with the address and message.

And then his expression changed again. Cara saw his eyes narrow. He moved the card slightly. And muttered something under his breath.

He'd seen it.

This time his gaze shot to her face. "The postmark," he said.

"I know," she answered. "That's the main reason I wanted you to see it."

"The date."

"Yes."

She let out a breath she hadn't realized she'd been holding. His reaction, that sudden, tense alertness, told her that her own response hadn't been out of line.

Hope had mailed this postcard from a small mountain village

that, as far as she knew, Hope had never been to or even mentioned.

And she'd mailed it on the day she disappeared.

Chapter 3

"So you don't think I'm crazy?"

Gabe looked at the woman seated across from him. She looked like she belonged here, he thought. The little mouse was definitely gone, and this woman exuded a quiet sort of class that befitted the subtle elegance and style of the Redstone flagship.

He gave himself a mental shake; he knew he was rattled when he spent so much time dwelling on the presence of a woman he'd known for years instead of the stunning bit of the past he held in his hand.

"Crazy?" he asked.

"For thinking this—" she gestured at the postcard "—means something. More than just the post office needs a little work."

He smiled at the quip, grateful to her for lightening the mood a bit. But the truth of what she said was undeniable, as was the weight of it. They now knew what they'd never been able to determine before, where Hope had gone that day. Or at least, the direction she'd gone.

"We never even got close to looking here," he said, tapping the card against his palm.

"There was no reason to," Cara said reasonably. "Hope wasn't a mountain wilderness, back-to-nature kind of person. She never even mentioned this place, at least not to me."

"Or me," Gabe said.

"I..." She stopped, and he shifted his gaze to her face. For the first time he saw a trace of the old, hesitant girl he'd remembered.

"What?"

"I wasn't sure you'd even want to know, after all this time."

"Want to know? Whether my wife was abducted, killed or just plain walked out on me?"

The words burst from him so fervently it startled him. It had always been there for the last eight years, this gnawing question, but he thought he'd managed to successfully blunt the edges of it by keeping it buried deep.

Apparently not, he thought wryly.

"Why on earth would she have walked out on you?"

"For someone else?" he suggested.

"Oh, please."

Cara seemed sincerely astonished at the idea, which mollified his fervor and soothed the tangled emotions he didn't like admitting to.

"You don't think so?" He hadn't really been convinced himself, if for no other reason than Hope had never contacted her parents. Even knowing they wouldn't have approved of an affair, he couldn't picture her leaving them worrying endlessly.

"Hardly. She was foolish sometimes, but not a fool."

That surprised him; he'd thought Cara considered Hope the feminine ideal, in the way somewhat plain girls sometimes idolized their more glamorous sisters. Not that Cara was plain, at least, certainly not anymore.

"We'd had our...moments," he said, somewhat hastily.

"I know that. But I also know she was happy, in those last days. Very."

"When I told her I was leaving the navy, she…seemed that way. She called it…a miracle," he said, only now realizing she'd used the word on that postcard as well. But what was the second miracle she'd written about?

Cara gave him a look then that he couldn't quite interpret. It seemed almost sad, although about what he couldn't guess.

"She *was* happy," she said. "I know that card seems like her same old griping about you being gone, but she really had lightened up about it, after you said you were leaving. I couldn't believe it."

His brow furrowed as he looked at her. "You couldn't believe what?"

"I was…shocked. I never thought you'd really do it. I thought you loved the navy."

Those quiet words jabbed at him. He looked down at the card, not to read it again—he already had the words committed to memory—but in order not to look at Cara and see the look he now recognized as pity, or something close enough to it that it rankled.

"I never thought you'd give in to her…whining."

Whining? An odd word for her to use to describe her best friend's discontent, he thought, and his gaze flicked back to her face.

"Is that what you think? That I quit because my wife nagged me into it?"

"It seemed that way." She had the grace to look uncomfortable. "On the surface," she added, in a conciliatory tone.

"Thanks for that much," he muttered.

"You're still in uniform, of a sort," she said.

He glanced down at the red polo shirt he wore, with the Redstone logo—a graphic of the *Hawk I*, the small jet that had begun an empire—on the left chest. Paired with crisp khakis, just as the rest of the crew wore, it was a uniform without looking like one.

"Josh doesn't go in much for formality."

"I've read about him," she said. "He seems almost too good to be true."

Grateful for the change of subject, Gabe nodded. "Anybody

else, I'd probably agree with you. Not Josh. He started with nothing and built Redstone the hard way, one brick at a time, with his own hands. One person at a time, with his own judgment."

She studied him for a moment. "You're happy here," she finally said.

"Yes," he agreed. "I've got a great boat under me, and better, I answer to a man I respect completely."

It was as close as he'd come to the real reason he'd left the navy, and he wasn't about to come any closer with this woman he hadn't seen in years.

He turned his attention back to the postcard. "It was mailed at eleven-twenty, according to the postage label meter. About the time it would take to get up there if she left where we lived then in San Diego at nine."

"And Hope rarely got herself moving to go anywhere before nine," Cara agreed.

This third dig was too much for Gabe to ignore. "I always had the idea Hope could do no wrong in your book."

Cara shrugged. "Time was," she said. "But a funny thing happened. I grew up."

Gabe's breath caught as she put her finger on the very thing that had always bothered him; Hope hadn't seemed inclined to do that at all. She'd wanted the carefree life she'd always had, and hadn't been happy with one reality had presented her. But she'd been so alive and vibrant that everyone had accepted it as just part of her unique charm.

"Don't get me wrong," Cara hastened to add, "I love her. She was the sister I never had, and I'll always feel that way about her."

Gabe noticed the confusion of present and past tense, but didn't comment; he'd felt that way too often himself to make an issue of it. And more than once, in the dark of night, he had faced his inner-most thoughts, admitted to the silence that it would be easier to know she'd left him. That she'd met someone who could give her the full-time attention she wanted. At least then he could be angry, or hurt, or stir up some righteous indignation. Something. Anything.

Hell, it would even be easier to know she was dead than to live forever in this limbo.

"What about you, Gabe?"

The question startled him out of the grim reverie. "What?"

"I was surprised when I talked to Hope's parents. I'd assumed you'd have taken the legal steps by now. To have her declared dead, I mean. It's been long enough, hasn't it?"

"Death in absentia?" Gabe said, his mouth twisting into a humorless smile. "A very inconclusive ending."

"But necessary, for you to go on with your life."

"I'm here and alive, aren't I?"

There was pure curiosity in her look then. "But...haven't you ever wanted...I mean, hasn't there been someone, in all this time, that made you want to—"

"No."

There had been, in fact, women in his life. Briefly. But when the subject of his status arose, that usually brought things to a quick end. He wondered how many of those women suspected he'd had something to do with his wife's disappearance and had run for their lives. He couldn't blame them, not really; too often it was the truth, and none of them had gotten to know him well enough to trust in his innocence. The fact that he'd been half a world away aboard an amphibious assault ship had been a pretty unassailable personal alibi, but there were conspiracy theorists everywhere, too many of them writing the news, it seemed.

And in the end, he hadn't cared enough to pursue it. That part of him seemed numb, and he wasn't sure he didn't like it that way.

"Do you think it would be worth looking into?"

Again her question snapped him out of the unpleasant thoughts. He wasn't usually one to get lost in his head like this, and it bothered him that he was now. It had to be Cara, he thought. Just her presence, so familiar and yet so changed, that had his mind spinning into all these old, dark places.

"Do you even want to?" Cara asked after a moment when he didn't speak.

Her tone was even, non-judgmental, and he had the feeling that if he said no, she'd accept it. And if she thought less of him for it, she would never let it show. Not just because she'd always kept her thoughts to herself, although she had, but because he sensed the classy demeanor was real, not just a facade.

"Is it worth it?" He echoed her words, running them through his head.

"I don't know. My first thought was to call the police. But I couldn't drag it all up again, if it's going to come to nothing. Hope's parents…"

Her voice trailed off. He knew exactly what she meant, and slowly shook his head. The memory of the pain in those much-loved, worn faces made his chest tighten.

"They've been through enough," he said.

She nodded. "Calling them, telling them, was so hard. They took it so hard…I didn't know what to do. So instead of calling the police, I came to you."

Something in her voice made his chest tighten even more. "Why?"

It was out before he thought, and he wondered why he'd asked, when in fact it didn't really matter why she'd come here. She had, and it was in his lap now.

"Because no one has a bigger stake in this than you," she said simply.

"Yours is pretty big," he pointed out. "She was your best friend for most of your life."

"Yes," she agreed. "But she was your wife. It doesn't get any bigger than that."

Oddly, it was her assessment of the marriage relationship that he focused on, rather than the old ache of speaking of Hope in the past tense. Interesting, he thought. And wondered again if she'd married somewhere along the line. And then, suddenly, he was asking her.

"Did you marry someone, Cara?"

She looked startled at the sudden shift. But she answered, with the direct honesty he'd always remembered, the honesty he was glad hadn't been glossed over by the more sophisticated appearance.

"No. I was engaged. He was killed."

In seven short words she made him regret he'd ever asked, wish he'd smothered his curiosity.

"I'm sorry."

"Me, too. He was a nice guy."

He wondered if he should ask what had happened, now that he'd lifted the lid on that box of troubles.

"It's all right," she said, her voice still even. "It was six years ago. It's not…raw, anymore."

Six years. Fairly soon after Hope had vanished. Connection? he wondered. Had she gone looking for comfort and found it in some…nice guy's arms?

None of your business, he told himself. And gestured abruptly with the card.

"I'm not sure this is enough to go to the police with, not after all this time."

"I wasn't sure, either," she said. "But it seemed as if I should do…something."

He looked again at the postmark, at the date and time that would be a marker in his life for as long as he lived. Could he really pass up the chance to get answers? Perhaps too much time had passed, perhaps nothing would come of it, but could he really just walk away, hand this card to Cara and pretend he'd never seen it, that this message from the past had never arrived at all?

He knew he couldn't. His gaze flicked back to Cara's face, and he suddenly knew she couldn't, either. If he said no, she would accept it, but she wouldn't walk away from it herself. She wouldn't forget, wouldn't even try. He wasn't sure how or why he was so certain of it, but he was. Maybe he'd known the little mouse better than he'd realized; tenacity had always been one of her qualities, he thought now.

"I just don't know what I could do," she said. "The police, they have resources, ways of checking on things, that I don't have."

He wondered for the first time what she was doing these days. He vaguely remembered she'd been a business and marketing major in college, and wondered what that had translated into in a real-life career.

And then her words stirred up something in his head.

They have resources, ways of checking on things, Cara had said of the police.

…if you need anything, if Redstone can help, call.

Josh's words echoed, and Gabe suddenly realized that while he wasn't the police, he certainly had some sizable and impressive resources at his disposal. Maybe even Redstone Security, the much-vaunted and incredibly effective private security force that had grown along with Redstone to handle problems around the world. He'd heard stories he wouldn't have believed were he outside Redstone, of things they'd done, operations they'd pulled off, all without stepping on the toes of law enforcement. In fact, he'd heard they were the envy of cops wherever they went, for both their freedom and those resources.

And wouldn't it just figure, he thought, if the job he'd taken in near desperation while floundering in the aftermath of his wife's disappearance, turned out to be the instrument of his finally discovering what had happened to Hope?

"Let me make a call," he told Cara.

He took his cell phone out of his back pocket.

He was about to find out if all the stories were true.

Chapter 4

"Expected you."

Gabe blinked. "You did?" he said into the phone.

"Josh said."

St. John's terseness was legendary at Redstone, and anyone who'd dealt with Josh's right-hand man had had to learn to translate. But he was so incredible at what he did, so efficient, and had sources Gabe figured even Josh didn't know—or want to know—about, that no one was about to quibble that they had to pay extra close attention to follow his extraordinary verbal leaps.

"Already?" Josh had only left here this morning.

St. John didn't answer. Gabe supposed his comment didn't require one; he should have known Josh wouldn't dally if he thought one of his own might need help.

"A list?" St. John asked.

Gabe shook his head, thinking dealing with St. John as liaison was going to be interesting. Technically, his title was vice-president of operations, but anyone who'd been around very long knew there were few aspects of Redstone St. John didn't know more about than seemed humanly possible.

"Not yet, not really. All I need right now is some info on Pine Lake, California. It's a little town up in the San Bernardino mountains. Near Lake Arrowhead."

"Target?"

This seemed oddly familiar, Gabe thought as he answered. "I'm trying to backtrack someone from a postcard that was mailed eight years ago."

If St. John thought he was crazy, he kept it to himself, as it was rumored he did most things.

"Going yourself?" was all he said.

"Yes. Shortly."

"This your cell?"

"Yes."

Gabe stifled a lopsided smile as he stopped himself from giving the number St. John no doubt already had from caller ID. The other part of his reputation was that he had little patience for people who belabored the obvious.

"Before you get there."

"Uh...thanks," Gabe said, his hesitation marking the time it took him to realize St. John had hung up without another word.

"Who was that?" Cara asked.

"St. John. Josh Redstone's right arm."

She lifted a brow. "You look...taken aback."

"I am," he admitted. "He's a little like listening to a machine gun."

And suddenly he had it, the source of that familiarity. It had been like the old days in the navy, on war games or training exercises; the more tense or dangerous things got, the fewer words were spoken. Commands, reports, decisions, they all got shorter, sharper and tenser.

"He talks," Gabe mused aloud, "like he's at war."

"Perhaps he is," Cara said.

Gabe focused on her then. "What?"

She lifted one shoulder in a half-shrug that echoed his own earlier one. "There's more than one kind of war, isn't there?"

Gabe thought of his own personal war, with the memories of Hope and the questions she'd left in her wake. "Yes," he said, acknowledging her insight with a nod. "Yes, there is."

"So, we're going to Pine Lake?"

He blinked. "We?" He'd thought he'd just head up there, ask some questions, poke around a little. He hadn't intended on having company.

"You did say I have a big stake in this. And the card came to me."

He couldn't argue with that, so didn't try. "All right," he said. "Let me go change clothes."

As he went to the spacious cabin allotted to the captain of this latest Redstone boat, a space that managed to be luxurious and utilitarian at the same time, he didn't wonder if he was going to regret this. He already knew he would.

He just wondered how much.

"Sorry for the delay. I had to leave some orders with the first mate."

Cara, who had been standing before a glass case, studying the intricately detailed, one-eighth scale model of the boat she was now standing on and marveling at the kind of mind that could take something like this from idea to reality, glanced at her watch before she turned. It was only a little after one.

"Not a problem, we have…plenty of time."

She thought she covered her quick intake of breath fairly well as she turned and saw him. Well enough, she hoped.

Gabriel Taggert in naval uniform had been stunning. In the more casual Redstone attire, he'd been extremely attractive.

In snug jeans and a long-sleeved dark gray T-shirt he was sexy as hell.

He frowned suddenly. Cara's next breath caught; had he seen her reaction after all, had he somehow guessed what simply looking at him had done to her pulse rate?

"Do you have a jacket or sweater or something?"

She knew she must be looking like an idiot, staring blankly at him, but she was having trouble making the shift from contemplating flat abs and the appeal of back pockets to the mundane question.

"What?"

"It's warm here, but it'll be cooler up in the mountains. It's only March, and it might be in the forties or so. Could even still be snow around."

"Oh. No, I don't."

She felt even more foolish now; she should have realized a man like Gabe wouldn't waste any time, but would want to do whatever could be done and do it now. She should have come prepared.

He turned and walked back down the hallway he'd apparently come out of. She had a moment to appreciate the view, but quickly made herself turn away, not wanting to get caught gaping at him.

But when he came back and tossed her a soft, fleecy sort of zipper jacket that had the Redstone logo embroidered on the front, it was something else that sent her reeling; it was his. She knew it was, because she could smell the faintest trace of the clean-scented aftershave she'd always associated with him.

God, you're hopeless!

She'd meant to chide herself out of her stupid meanderings, but instead it sounded, even in her head, pitiful.

"I meant to ask," she said hastily as she resisted lifting the jacket to her face for a deeper breath, "you were wearing the same thing as the rest of the crew. No special uniform for the captain?"

His mouth quirked. "Yeah. I get to wear a ball cap with the boat's silhouette stitched on it."

"Oh."

"Sorry, no scrambled eggs."

He remembers, Cara thought with a start. *He actually remembers.*

It was one of her most vivid memories, that day when he'd sailed out and she'd gone with Hope to see him off. It had been only the second or third time she'd met the new man in Hope's life. He'd been wearing one version—she hadn't known there were so many kinds—of a dress uniform and in her ignorance of things military, she'd asked him what all the gold on his visor was.

He'd grinned at her, and explained. And she'd promptly fallen for him.

And apparently she'd never gotten around to standing up again.

"Seat belt," Gabe said absently.

"Got it."

Cara shifted in the seat of the low-slung coupe; the Lexus was a nice change from her little compact, and it was pure luxury to be able to completely stretch out her legs. They had decided, since he knew how to get to where they were going, that he'd drive. Once she'd seen the sleek, dark blue car, she was glad she had agreed. She wondered if he had trouble with other cars, as tall as he was.

"Nice car," she said now. "Redstone pays well, obviously." She'd heard that anyway, but it was hard not to comment on it when she was sitting in the evidence.

"It does," Gabe said. "But it's not just that. There's another, financial benefit to working for Redstone."

"What's that?"

"Mac McClaren."

Cara's brows shot up. "The gazillionaire treasure hunter?"

"And the guy who gave Josh his start, when all he had was a pilot's license, a design in his head and a dream. That Spanish galleon he found helped build the foundation of Redstone." Gabe smiled. "Of course, he's pouring money into his wife's pet cause now. There are a lot of homeless animals eating better these days."

"I didn't realize he was connected to Redstone."

"Most people don't. But the man's a lot more than a treasure hunter. He did that mainly to prove his father had been right about where that ship had gone down. He's also a financial genius, and he's at the disposal of anybody who works for Redstone. Including—" he gestured at the interior of the car, the rich leather, the polished wood "—me."

"Nice perk," she said.

"One of the benefits of working for a guy who makes friends for life," Gabe said.

She looked at him curiously. "Is he? A friend, I mean? Is that how you ended up there?"

"He is now," Gabe said, "but I didn't even know him when he offered me my first job at Redstone."

"How'd that happen?" she asked, intrigued now. "It's not like you see advertisements for them."

He chuckled. "No, Josh doesn't have to advertise. People are lined up literally around the world wanting to work for him."

She noticed he hadn't actually answered her. "So, how?" she persisted.

When he hesitated, then let out a compressed breath, she knew she hadn't imagined that he had been dodging her question.

"He'd read about the…incident that made me quit the navy. He was angry. Asked some of those friends he has about it, friends in or with connections to the military. My name came up."

There was a flatness in his tone that made her remember their earlier conversation.

I never thought you'd give in to her…whining.

Is that what you think? That I quit because my wife nagged me into it?

"Why did you really quit, Gabe?"

"Hope, remember?" She'd irritated him now. Or he was still irritated by her earlier assumption.

"Hope was…a very social person," she began, needing to say something, anything.

"Yes," Gabe acknowledged. "And she needed someone who could be there for that kind of thing, social occasions. I couldn't give her that, not the way she wanted."

"But…she knew that, going in. She had to."

"She thought she could deal with it." He lifted a hand from the polished mahogany steering wheel to the back of his neck, rubbed as if it were aching. "She couldn't. Long deployments take a huge toll. It takes an incredibly strong person to be a military spouse, in the best of times."

"I can only imagine," she said softly.

And *strong* was not a word Cara would use to describe Hope. Beautiful, vivacious, energetic, impulsive, yes, but strong? No. Not when she remembered all the seemingly endless phone calls where Hope had whined—not a flattering word, but the only one that really fit—about her husband's absence. As if he had chosen to leave, as if he'd abandoned her intentionally.

He lapsed into silence, apparently focused on driving although traffic was light. She waited, and when they'd pulled to a halt at a stop light, quietly asked again.

"Why did you really quit?"

He turned his head. Her breath stopped in her chest. She'd never seen him look this way before. He'd always seemed intense to her, but there was something in his eyes now that made her almost afraid to move.

It took her a moment to realize what she was seeing; there was more of the military officer left in Gabriel Taggert than she'd thought. This was the kind of man who did what others were afraid to, who knew things, did things, went places the average person going about their comfortable life never had to think about, precisely because there were men like Gabe in the world, willing and able to do it for them.

It was only with great effort that she managed not to look away from that fierce gaze.

"I quit," he said in measured tones that hinted at a lingering anger, "after twenty-three good, honest, heroic people died because some *politicians*—" he snarled the word "—decided it would upset the balance of power in the entire world if they were warned about an attack on them in time to defend themselves."

Cara smothered a gasp. "They could have warned them? And didn't?"

He looked away then, back to the front as the light changed, as if even now he was completely aware of his surroundings.

When he went on, his voice was quieter, but she didn't mistake that for calm.

"They chose not to, knowing what would happen. They didn't just let them die, they sacrificed them on the altar of political expediency. They died, horribly, without ever knowing why." He sucked in an audible breath. "Which may have been better than knowing the truth."

Judging by the fact that he was still angry after all these years, she tended to agree with that.

"I didn't know, Gabe. I'm...I don't know what I am. Sick, maybe. That something like that could happen. Be allowed to happen." She hesitated, then made herself ask. "The ones who died...they were your people?"

He flicked her a sideways glance. "They were navy," he said.

The words were simple, but they spoke volumes about the man. And told her that everything she'd ever thought about him was true.

Chapter 5

"I'm sorry, Gabe. For ever thinking you'd quit your career for…anything less than something like that."

He glanced at her again. Her words had surprised him. Not as much as the fact that he'd told her what he just had, when he rarely spoke of it at all, but she'd still surprised him.

"I would have thought you'd expect me to quit, if Hope demanded it."

Her mouth quirked. "There was a time when I suppose I might have," she said. "I'm not particularly proud of that at the moment. Hope's demands seem rather petty stacked up against the real reason you left."

That surprised him, too. Perhaps he'd gotten used to thinking Hope's version of what a woman needed was the only one.

"So how did Redstone happen, then?" Cara asked.

He'd told her so much already, there didn't seem to be any reason not to give her the rest. He kept his eyes on the road now that they were on the freeway, but his peripheral vision was as good as it had been in the navy, and he could see her fairly clearly.

"Somebody he knew told Josh I'd quit, and why. He tracked me down. Offered me a job running his maritime division. I took it." She saw one corner of his mouth curve up slightly. "Saved my life, after Hope."

He said it lightly, in an effort to negate the intensity of the past few minutes.

"I should have been in touch more, then," she said, as if she suspected there was more truth in the words than his tone admitted to. "I was so caught up in my own grief at the time I was afraid I'd break down sobbing every time, and I didn't think you'd appreciate a weepy woman pestering you. Besides, I—"

She stopped suddenly and looked down at her hands in her lap. He risked a glance then, and he saw that her cheeks were pink. He let a moment pass while he turned his focus back to the roadway.

"You what?"

"At the time, I'd never been in love, not really, so I didn't really realize what it feels like to have the one person you love most ripped out of your life without warning."

"And now you do."

He said it softly, and it wasn't a question.

"Yes."

"Who was he, Cara?"

"His name was Robert. He was a police officer. Killed in the line of duty, during an armed robbery. He got between the robber and a little girl."

She recited it as if it were a speech she'd memorized. He imagined it probably was; it was easier to answer the inevitable questions if you had an answer packaged and ready, one that you didn't have to think about. He knew that from his own miserable experience.

"I'm sorry. We lose too many good guys."

He meant it, and tried to let it show in his voice. When she looked at him, and gave him a smile he realized she didn't think he could see, he knew she'd gotten it.

"Yes, we do. And he was definitely one of them."

He let a moment pass, in silent tribute to a man he would never know, before he said quietly, "I wouldn't have minded you calling, Cara. Even crying. Especially crying."

He glimpsed her sudden, startled look out of the corner of his eye, sensed her sudden stillness. And wondered what his wife had told her that had made her assume he would want nothing to do with someone because they were grief-stricken and expressing it in the most common way.

He felt a little jab of guilt at the thought; Hope was gone, and the arrival of this much-delayed postcard didn't change that. He shouldn't be having negative thoughts about her. Hope hadn't been perfect, he knew that, but he'd loved her, been captivated by her easy charm and vivacious beauty. And the fact that she had loved him had been flattering in a way, even if now he wasn't sure exactly what she'd loved.

"I wanted to," she admitted. "Except for Hope's parents, you were the only one I knew who was hurting as much as I was, but I didn't want to make it worse for you."

The thought that she'd worried about that, even then, touched him, more deeply than he ever would have expected. Disconcerted, he seized on the first thing that came to mind.

"We can't tell them what we're doing," he said. "Gwen and Earl, I mean. It may—likely will—come to nothing."

"Of course we can't. We have to do it, I couldn't rest if we didn't. But I wouldn't raise their hopes for anything, when it's all so…nebulous."

Her words stabbed at him, and his voice was tight when he spoke again. "It's new ground in the search," he admitted. "But you're not thinking we're going to find her up there, are you?"

Cara blinked. "Hope? You mean…alive? God, no."

He breathed again; he'd always suspected little, shy Cara lived a great deal in her mind, and for a moment he'd feared she might have built some kind of fantasy in her head about finding her dearest friend alive and well.

"In the beginning," she said, in the tone of an embarrassed admission, "I wondered. I used to lie awake at night, picturing Hope living a new life somewhere, maybe with a new name, like she'd seen something and ended up in witness protection, maybe with amnesia, silly things like that."

It was so close to what he'd been worried she was thinking he was disconcerted all over again. Perhaps he'd known her better than he'd realized.

"Not silly, under the circumstances," he said, all the while glad she knew now the thoughts had been seriously implausible.

"I know that, now. Grief does crazy things to you. Coupled with uncertainty, it's almost unbearable." She took in an audible breath. "That's why I know we can't say anything to Hope's parents. It's not that I'm expecting to find her, but if we could find out what happened to her, it might…not *help*, nothing can, but at least they'd know."

"Closure?"

He hated the word; it made him think of people expect you to pick up and go on as if nothing had happened once the funeral was over, because you had *closure*. But now he was beginning to wonder. Cara had lost someone, too, and she'd clearly managed to get past it. Was the difference just that, that she'd had closure, where he was left forever wondering?

She shrugged. "I'm not much for buzzwords like that, but there's something to the theory, I think. Especially when it's something like this, where you simply don't know what happened. It's too easy to slip over the edge and start clinging to thoughts like I had in the beginning, to slide into the madness of believing them."

Her words hung there between them for a moment while he negotiated a traffic slowdown for a stalled vehicle on the center divider of the freeway. When they were clear, he glanced over at her.

"You don't think the Waldrons are doing that, do you?"

"No. For all her sweet acquiescence, Gwen is a strong woman. She wouldn't, and wouldn't let Earl, either."

Gabe couldn't have agreed more with that assessment. And her easy statement of it reminded him once more of the quiet girl who would never have spoken of someone of her parents' generation in such a way. "You've really gone and grown up, haven't you?"

She smiled then, a flashing, bright expression that nearly stopped his heart in his chest.

"It happens," she said, her tone so teasing he couldn't help smiling back.

And just like that the mood in the car changed, from a rather edgy tension to an easy camaraderie he was thankful for; it was much easier to handle.

When they started up the mountain highway called the Rim of the World—for obvious reasons, given the curves and steep drop-offs that marked every mile—they were talking like the old, fairly close friends they'd been. He asked about her own parents, found out they were living in Oregon, where her father was headed toward a happy retirement of endless fishing and her mother was building yet another of the beautiful gardens she was known for. She asked about his father in turn, and smiled when he told her the admiral was still as gruff and feisty as ever at sixty-one, and running his staff ragged down in San Diego.

"He never remarried, after your mother died?"

"No. He says there's not another woman on the planet who would put up with him the way Mom did. Having lived with him myself, I tend to think he might be right."

She laughed, and an unexpected warmth flooded him again.

Strange, he thought. He never would have thought seeing quiet little Cara Thorpe again would stir up so much emotion in him. True, she'd been a big part of his life for a while, although always on the edges, and he'd accepted her at first because he loved Hope and she was her best friend. But later he'd come to like the quiet girl for herself, enjoyed trying to gently nudge her out of her shyness, to get her to open up and talk to him.

He'd seen flashes of a different Cara back then, times when she'd surprised him with a cogent, astute observation about something that had made him realize she was indeed the personification of still waters running deep. But he'd been wrapped up in first true love, and hadn't thought much beyond that about the girl who was the quiet shadow of the lively, vivid Hope Waldron.

Cara Thorpe now would stand in no one's shadow, he thought suddenly. Not in looks, demeanor, or personality. She—

The ring of his cell interrupted his thoughts. He hit the button on the hands-free system built into the controls of the Lexus.

"Taggert."

"Smallest village in the county. No sheriff's substation. Two restaurants, one twenty-room motel, some touristy stuff. Post Office in the back of the general store. Same person running it for thirty years. Anson Woodruff. Town gossip. He's there now."

Gabe stifled a grin at St. John's clipped, concise report, and at Cara's bemused expression as the man's brusque voice sounded in the car.

"Thank you," he said.

"More?"

"Not yet. I'll let you know."

The click was audible as the connection was severed.

"I gather that was…the machine gun?" Cara said.

"It was."

"I see what you mean. He's always like that?"

"I don't know for sure. This is the first time I've dealt with him at any length on the phone."

"Surely he's not like that in person?"

"No, he's mostly silent," Gabe said, still grinning. "At least, he has been the few times I've met him. He's got quite the reputation for being a man of no words. So when he does talk, you'd best listen."

"He seemed…efficient in the extreme."

"That's the other part of the reputation," Gabe said. "Josh says if you ever hear him talking normally, look out. That's when he's the most dangerous."

"Dangerous? Odd word for a business executive, isn't it?"

"Not when you meet him."

She seemed to ponder this for a moment. But when she spoke again, it was about their destination.

"We start with Anson Woodruff?" she asked.

"Seems the most logical. Let's hope he has a good memory."

Cara smiled. "In my admittedly limited small-town experience, it seems town gossips usually do."

He laughed, and even as he did he marveled a little that he could, given the mission they were on.

And it was a mission, he couldn't deny that. That he was on it with the most unlikely of people didn't change that.

No matter how much Cara Thorpe had changed.

Chapter 6

Mr. Woodruff, as it turned out, all seventy-two years of him, had an excellent memory.

And absolutely no problem with sharing everything in it, without even asking who they were or why they wanted to know. The problem, Gabe soon realized, was in keeping him on the track they wanted.

"That was the summer the old roadhouse burned down," he was saying now, rubbing a hand over his bald head as if it were a long-standing habit. "Never seen such a fuss, although if you ask me, it was no great loss. Place had turned into a dive, nothing but drunks and pool players every night. Firemen had to go in and pull those sorry drunks out. And we only have a volunteer fire department you know, they're not—"

"It must have been awful," Cara said, just as Gabe was about to impatiently yank the man back to their original question. "Was this before or after you saw Hope?"

"Your friend?" the man asked, as if it had been hours ago, not ten minutes, when they'd first come in to ask.

"Yes," Cara said patiently.

Gabe himself was ready to snap, *Yes, the only reason we came in here!* but realized Cara's approach was much more likely to be productive.

"Oh, before," Mr. Woodruff said. "She came in the very next day. Lovely young woman. I told her all about the fire, she was very interested."

I'll bet you did, Gabe thought. He let Cara continue; if the old gent preferred to talk to another lovely young woman, far be it for him to interfere.

"How did she seem to you?"

"Seem? Why, a pretty young girl. Charming, just charming. She bought that card, went over to the café to write it, then came back and mailed it."

"So she wasn't…upset, or distraught, anything like that?"

Mr. Woodruff drew back slightly, his thick, bushy gray brows lowered. "Upset? Why, no, she didn't seem to be. In fact, she seemed very happy, excited even. Bubbly," he added, smiling.

That was Hope, all right, Gabe thought. Except when she was upset at his long absences, she'd always been that way.

"You're sure?" he asked.

"My memory," Mr. Woodruff said primly, "is razor-sharp."

Yeah, he definitely preferred talking to Cara, Gabe thought. *Can't blame the old guy for that.*

Cara asked quickly, "She didn't seem like she was unhappy, or frightened or anything?"

Mr. Woodruff frowned at that. "No, not at all. And I would have remembered, I think. I don't like seeing pretty ladies in distress."

He gave Cara a smile Gabe was sure was supposed to be charming in turn. The man was a flirt, Gabe realized suddenly, and had to hide a smile as his irritation vanished.

Cara chatted on for a few more minutes while Gabe inwardly laughed at himself; after eight years, he was suddenly in a hurry?

So Hope had been happy. He hadn't been wrong about that.

But they were no closer to knowing why she'd been here in this little hamlet to begin with. Or what had happened after she'd come in here, bought that postcard, scrawled her hasty, excited message on it, and dropped it in the mail.

It was very Hope-like, that after calling and being unable to reach her friend, that she would write something. She was always scribbling things down, and had kept journals she'd made him swear on his honor never to snoop into. He'd kept his word, although he'd let the police look through them when she'd first vanished. They hadn't been much help, since they'd ended about the time she'd gotten her new laptop computer, and he assumed she'd begun to keep her journals electronically.

At last Cara bid the affable Mr. Woodruff goodbye, and they turned away from the postal counter in the back of the store. It was one of those small, old places that nevertheless seemed to have everything you could possibly need. A little expensive, although not exorbitant given what it probably cost to keep the place supplied; not a lot of variety, but all the essentials were there, from fresh produce to souvenir T-shirts to spark plugs. Gabe imagined the locals both avoided it and welcomed its presence, depending on how desperate they were to avoid a trip down the mountain road to other shopping options.

The old wooden floor creaked as they walked, and it was an oddly comforting sound. Cara paused to smile at a display of chain saw parts next to stacked bundles of kindling.

"The implication being if you buy the one you don't need the other, I suppose," Gabe said.

Cara grinned at that. "Good marketing."

Gabe glanced back at Mr. Woodruff's domain, where the man was gesturing widely as he told another story to yet another captive listener, a woman with a small child in her arms. No wonder he'd lasted thirty years there; it was the perfect venue for him to have a constant, rotating audience.

"I'm glad you thought to bring that photograph," Gabe said as they continued through the store.

"It's always in my wallet. I know it's of both of us, but it's clear enough of her."

"Yes. He recognized her right away. She hadn't changed much, since then."

He didn't point out that Cara herself was barely recognizable as the same woman.

"No, she hadn't. Even though it's almost eleven years old." She paused, then said in a voice that seemed quite different, "It's the one you took. In La Jolla that time."

It took him a moment, but he finally remembered. "Your joint birthday bash."

She smiled, seeming pleased he'd remembered. "Yes."

His ship had been in port in San Diego for some refitting work, and Hope had been deliriously happy that he was going to be around for several months. So happy that it infected everyone around her, even quiet Cara, who had joined in the fun wholeheartedly when, at Hope's insistence, they went out for dinner at Hope's favorite restaurant. Hope had always been good at that, loved planning things down to the last detail. And she'd always been generous with her friends, Cara most of all.

He even remembered the moment when he'd snapped the shot; the two had posed at the beach park, on the bluff above the rocky, sheltered cove that was one of the seaside community's major attractions.

It was also the day he'd asked Cara why she didn't like him.

"I always wondered if you were mad at me."

It was out before he thought. And Cara looked so astonished, he knew he'd been wrong about that before she even answered him.

"Mad? Why would I have been mad at you?"

"I married your best friend. She didn't have as much time with you after that, when I was around."

"But you included me so often," she said, a slight urgency in her voice that puzzled him. Her next words explained the tone to him. "And you never, ever made me feel like...like a fifth wheel. I never thanked you for that. Not many men would have put up with Hope wanting me along so much."

"I never thought of you like that, a fifth wheel," Gabe said. "I was glad she had a friend like you, to rely on when I couldn't be there for her."

"Well," Cara said wryly, "I could do that, since not much else was going on in my life, wallflower that I was."

"You were...quiet," he said, somewhat carefully.

She laughed, and it was a genuine one, light and pleasant. "That's an understatement."

"Obviously you outgrew it," he said, that laugh making him unable to stop himself from teasing her.

"I'll take that as a compliment."

"It was meant that way. You've really...blossomed," he finished a bit lamely; it sounded impossibly corny to his ears.

"That wouldn't have been hard. I was very...unsure of myself, back then."

"I thought you were just shy. Or like I said, didn't like me."

"I liked you." She looked away quickly, then back at him. He thought he heard her take a quick breath, and when she went on, her words came out quicker than usual. "Too much. I had a bit of a shy girl's crush on you."

Gabe stared at her. "You what?"

"I thought I did, anyway. It took me a while to realize it was mainly that I wanted what Hope had. The love, the feeling, not necessarily...the person."

It happened so fast Gabe could barely keep up, the astonishment at her admission, and the sudden refutation of it. To his amazement, he found himself feeling oddly disappointed when she explained she'd essentially been in love with the idea of what he and Hope had, not him.

This was a revelation he didn't quite know what to think about; he'd never thought of himself as the kind of man who needed women falling all over him. He'd wanted Hope, and he'd gotten her, and that had been more than enough, while the good part lasted. So why this sense of letdown because Cara Thorpe had decided she hadn't had a crush on him? Especially when he'd never known she even thought she had?

"So we know Hope was really here the day she disappeared, and she bought, wrote and mailed that card the same day."

Cara had obviously moved on, perhaps embarrassed by what she'd admitted. Since he wasn't at all sure how he felt about it, he welcomed the change of subject.

"Yes," he agreed. "But we still don't know why she was here."

"Or where to go from here," Cara said.

"Well, if she stopped here to get and mail that card, maybe she did something else, too. Let's ask around, maybe—"

"Hello?"

They both turned at the hesitant interruption. It was the woman who'd been after them at the postal counter. The child she held, a dark-haired little girl who looked about two, was dozing on her shoulder.

"I'm Laura Ginelli. Mr. Woodruff said you were asking about Hope Taggert."

Gabe and Cara exchanged a quick glance. He chose his words carefully, using present tense, for reasons he didn't stop to analyze. "You know her?"

"I haven't seen her in years, since she stopped coming up here."

Gabe went still. He knew Cara had picked up on the same thing he had, when she asked, "Stopped?"

"Yes. Without a word. I always thought that was strange, but she was kind of…flighty that way, my grandmother would say. No offense, if she's related to you or something."

"I'm Gabriel Taggert," Gabe said, watching the woman for a reaction.

"Oh! I should have guessed," Laura said with a flashing smile that lit up her dark eyes. "She said you were the personification of tall, dark and handsome."

Gabe blinked as Cara laughed. "Isn't he just?" she said to the woman.

Gabe was rarely at a complete loss for words, but he was now. Not that he didn't appreciate the compliments, but he was never sure how to deal with such open admiration. Was he supposed to say thank you, or what?

Fortunately, Cara saved him from the awkward moment. "I'm Cara Thorpe," she said to the woman. With a glance at Gabe, she added, "Hope...was my best friend."

He noted the change of tense, and agreed with her; this woman obviously had no idea anything unusual had happened. Cara quickly explained about the much-delayed postcard.

"Oh, you're the one she wrote to, then?" Laura said after marveling at the belated delivery. "I wondered who on earth she'd been sending a postcard of this little burg to, and she said she hadn't been able to reach you by phone."

"You seem to remember pretty well, for something so long ago," Gabe said, careful to keep his tone merely curious.

"I do," Laura said. "I'm good with that kind of thing, and besides, I remember because it was the last time I saw her, and I always wondered why she never came back."

"So you saw her that day?" Cara asked. "The day she mailed that card to me?"

Laura nodded, and gestured across the street to the small coffee shop they'd noticed when they arrived. "I used to work over there, until my older son was born. Hope would come in when she was in town, for a milkshake. She loved them, and they make them the old way, with a big blender, not out of a machine."

"Strawberry," Gabe said softly.

"Yes," Laura said with a smile. "Anyway, she came in for one, and was writing on a postcard. When she finished, we chatted a little, like always."

And then the smile faded as she looked at them. She seemed to realize finally that there was something not typical about their questions.

"Something's happened, hasn't it?"

"That day," Gabe said, his voice tight despite his efforts, "was the last day my wife was seen anywhere."

Chapter 7

Laura Ginelli gasped. "What?"

"She disappeared," Cara said, knowing there was no way to tactfully break such news. "No one's seen or heard from her since."

"But...that was years ago!"

"Yes."

"Oh, God, I was afraid of something like that."

"Why?" Gabe asked sharply, clearly wondering if the woman had reason to think something might have happened. But Laura's answer was much simpler.

"Because she loved it here, and it didn't seem like her to just stop coming without a word."

"The police looked for her for months, but no one knew to come up here," Cara said.

Laura frowned. She glanced at Gabe. "But...didn't you tell them?"

His jaw tightened. "I didn't know she'd ever set foot here."

Laura's gaze suddenly narrowed, as if she were pondering all the reasons Hope might not have told him about her apparently regular trips up here.

"Nor did I," Cara said quickly, sensing Gabe's reaction to the sudden suspicion in Laura's face. "Or her parents, as far as I know. For some reason, she kept her trips here a secret."

"Why would she do that?"

"That's what we'd like to know," Gabe said, his voice even tighter now. He looked strangely edgy, and Cara wondered if he hadn't expected this to hit him like this, not after all this time, or talking to people who had known Hope would make him so tense.

And she wondered how it was affecting him, finding out that there had been a side to his wife he'd known nothing about. She was shocked enough herself; she could only imagine how he must feel.

"Do you know…how long she'd been coming up here?" Cara asked.

"How long?" Laura seemed rattled by what they'd told her, and more than a little upset. "Let me think."

The little girl began to stir, and she shifted her against her hip. Funny, Cara thought inanely, how a woman could haul around twenty or thirty pounds or more of kid for hours and still be considered the weaker sex by some. Not to mention what they went through to get the kid here in the first place….

"At least a couple of years or so, off and on," Laura said at last. "She'd come every weekend for months, then not at all for months, then she'd be back." The young woman looked troubled; clearly she'd liked Hope. "I suppose that's why none of us realized she hadn't been back until a long time after that day."

It didn't take much thinking to figure out that Hope's trips up here likely correlated with Gabe's deployments; when he'd been home Cara knew Hope had never taken off for a weekend. She knew they'd spent every available minute together, until the time for his next departure approached, which was when she'd start getting moody again, calling Cara to complain.

The little girl woke up, opened eyes as dark as her mother's, saw she was among strangers, and promptly started to wail.

"Shh." Laura patted the little girl on the back, with no noticeable effect. "I need to feed her, and go pick up my son at school," she said. "I can't believe this. I'd just found out I was pregnant with him the last time I saw Hope. She was so excited for me. She said she was going to learn to knit so she could start making baby things."

"Thank you for talking with us," Cara said, trying without much luck to picture the energetic Hope settling down long enough to do something as calm as knitting.

"If you think of anything else," Gabe said, pulling out a business card with phone numbers on it, "would you call me? I'll be on the cell number for a while."

"Of course," she said, glancing at the card. "Redstone? So you really did leave the navy?"

"Yes." It was hard to talk over the yowling child, so Gabe left it at that.

"One other thing, if you could, before you go," Cara said. "Do you know why Hope started coming here? I mean, it's lovely up here and all, but we don't have any idea why here, specifically."

"To see her friend Miriam, I assume," Laura said, bouncing the child as if that would quiet her.

"Miriam?" Gabe asked, a little sharply; clearly this was something else he hadn't known about.

"Who is Miriam?" Cara asked.

"I'm afraid I don't know her last name. Hope just mentioned that she came here to see her. I don't think she lives right here in the village, because we're small and everyone knows everyone, and I didn't know the name."

The crying became a screech, and Laura apologized before heading off to deal with her hungry child, leaving Gabe and Cara standing on the sidewalk, both a little stunned by this development.

Cara looked at Gabe, who was looking after Laura Ginelli with an expression she couldn't define. But then, the man had just found out his wife, the woman he'd so loved, had apparently had a secret life and one he'd never known about, or even suspected.

She knew how she felt that her best friend had kept all this from her, but…the person you married, were supposed to share all with…how could Hope have kept this from Gabe?

Why on earth would she have walked out on you?

For someone else?

Their earlier exchange echoed in her ears, and for the first time she wondered. Just because she couldn't imagine anyone cheating on a man like Gabe….

"Rethinking whether she was having an affair?"

Gabe's quiet words yanked her out of her thoughts, unsettling her with their accuracy. He was looking at her curiously. She would have thought he'd have been more upset at having to seriously consider the idea, but if he was, it didn't show.

But then, hadn't Hope always said ramrod-straight Gabriel Taggert would never betray something like real emotion? Cara thought of his laughter earlier, when they'd talked about Mr. Woodruff before they'd met him. That was emotion, wasn't it?

Not to Hope, she realized. To Hope, emotion meant angst, anger or tears. She would have to think about that, later. Right now Gabe was studying her a little too intently for her comfort, awaiting an answer.

"For an instant," she finally admitted. "But no, I still can't believe it. For all her sometimes capricious nature, Hope wouldn't do that."

"I tend to agree," Gabe said, in an emotionless tone that had Cara wondering again about Hope's complaint. But then, it had been eight years. Eight years of not knowing, wondering, had to wear out even the strongest of emotions. "Not clandestinely, anyway," he added.

"Exactly," Cara said. "She might walk out on someone, but only after a confrontation where she was able to present her grievances in the most dramatic manner."

Gabe blinked. She saw the corners of his mouth twitch, as if he were fighting a smile. "That," he said after a moment, "would definitely be Hope."

Pleased at his reaction for reasons she didn't want to examine too closely, Cara looked around at the main street of this little alpine-styled village.

"Maybe," she said, "if Hope used the post office, and spent time at the café, she did other things here, too."

Gabe's expression changed then, became more intent. "Good point." He looked up and down the street. "Shall we split up, cover more ground faster?"

Military efficiency, Cara thought, smothering a smile of her own. "But I have the photo," she pointed out. "Besides, between us we have…a bigger data base on Hope. Better chance something might register as significant."

The look he gave her then was admiring. "I always knew you were smart."

"That's me," she said, looking away then as voices from other days rang in her ears.

That Cara Thorpe, she's such a bright girl, too bad she's got no personality.

The little Thorpe girl, she's very clever, but far too shy.

Cara, you can't spend the whole summer living in the library! It's time to have some fun!

That last had been Hope, her one true friend for most of her life, based on the simple good luck that she was lively, outgoing, generous, and happened to live across the street. By sheer force of her considerable will, Hope had pulled the shy, protesting Cara into at least the periphery of her much more exciting life.

If it hadn't been for Hope, Cara thought, I'd still be that painfully shy, reclusive girl. She made me see I didn't have to stay that way.

So this was the least she could do for her missing friend.

We'll find out what happened to you, girlfriend. Somehow.

"I haven't even asked," Gabe said, sounding a bit embarrassed. "What are you doing, these days?"

"Using that marketing degree of mine, actually."

"Doing?"

"I run the PR and advertising department of a Web design company. It was just county-wide when I started five years ago, but we went regional last year. We're doing well."

Gabe's eyes widened. She smiled; she was proud of what she'd accomplished, and didn't mind letting it show.

"Good for you," he said, and there was a sincerity in his tone that warmed her. "Are you ever sorry you didn't go for law school?"

"Lord, no," she said with a laugh. "That was only a passing aberration, and rarely does a day go by when I'm not glad to not be swimming in that."

"You said you wanted to clean up that pool."

"That," she said dryly, "was before I realized it didn't *want* to be cleaned up. Too many of them like it that way."

He didn't dispute her words, just gave her a crooked smile that made her heart do a silly flip. Just like it always had when Gabe had ever deigned to smile at her. Which, she had to admit, he'd done often enough. He'd never been anything less than kind to her; it was her own silly feelings that had tangled things up.

And all this silliness she was feeling now had to be just a holdover from those days. Because nothing had really changed. Even now, after all this time, even with her best friend long missing, in her mind one thing remained unchangeable.

Gabriel Taggert belonged to Hope.

Chapter 8

Gabe rubbed the back of his neck, frowning.

"Are you all right?"

He looked at Cara across the table when she spoke. They'd finished talking to everyone they found on one side of the admittedly fairly short main street of Pine Lake, then had stopped for a meal at the café where Laura Ginelli had once worked. It was an odd hour, too late for lunch, a bit early for dinner, but they were both hungry since they'd skipped lunch in the effort to get here as soon as possible.

They'd found out quickly that Cara had been right. Hope, while not a local, hadn't been unknown to the people of Pine Lake. Her outgoing nature and charm, her vivaciousness, had made her memorable in the little village. They found several people who had stories to tell of the charming young woman who had been so easy to talk to.

None of them, however, had any idea what might have happened to the visitor to their midst. Nor did anyone, so far, know of a woman named Miriam.

"Just edgy, I guess," he said as he quit rubbing. "It must be the small town. I keep feeling like we're being watched every step of the way."

"Maybe we are," Cara said. "Although you'd think they'd be used to the occasional stranger or tourist coming through. They seem to want to attract them."

The feeling he'd gotten had been more specific than that, as if the watcher was intent on them in particular, but since he had absolutely nothing but this damned itch at the back of his neck to support it, he said nothing more.

"It's a pretty place," Cara said. "I can see the appeal. All this fresh air, the look and smell of pine trees, the quietness."

"So can I," Gabe agreed. "What I can't see is the appeal of it to Hope."

"I've been wondering that myself," Cara said. "She was a city girl, through and through."

"And not a designer shoe store in sight," Gabe said wryly.

Cara laughed; Hope's obsession with shoes had been legend. He himself had dress shoes in brown and black, running shoes, an old pair of lace-up military-style boots he'd held on to from the old days and deck shoes. Hope had had thirty pairs of black shoes he couldn't tell any difference between.

He'd figured it was a benign-enough obsession, and if it kept her happy he didn't mind. Although when she started creeping toward four figures for a pair of what she called "essential black pumps," he had started to wonder.

And packing them up for donation when he'd finally left the house they'd lived in had been one of the hardest things he'd ever done.

But right now, he was wondering again why he had never noticed what a great laugh Cara had. Had he not noticed, or had she simply laughed so little before, that he hadn't had the chance to notice? Had she been that shy around him?

Which brought him back to her confession of having had a crush on him.

"What?" Cara asked, making him realize he must have been staring at her.

"I was just thinking," he said hastily. "Back to the old days, when Hope and I used to talk about setting you up with one of my buddies."

Her eyes widened and her cheeks flushed. "You what?"

He wished now he hadn't said it. Not the first time since she'd dropped back into his life that he'd spoken before thinking, he thought wryly.

"We wanted you to be happy. She always knew you'd... blossom if given half a chance, that you were just unsure of yourself." He smiled at her, much as he had back then, when he'd tried to silently buck her up when he sensed she was panicking over some unwanted attention. "Obviously she was right."

"I...thank you. But did she really ask you to do that? Like a blind date?"

He nodded. "She was always after me to set up something with somebody I liked and trusted."

"How...awkward for you. I'm sorry."

He shrugged, but his mind was running as if it were an over-clocked computer. It had been a little awkward, especially since he'd never managed to come up with anyone, which had made Hope impatient. But not nearly as awkward as the realization that had suddenly struck him now.

He remembered going through a mental list, and finding some reason to discard each possibility. Karl Linden had been high on the list until Gabe found out he'd cheated on his longtime girlfriend. Then he'd caught Jim Hardy in a lie about something inconsequential, which had made him wonder about his truthfulness in important things. Darrell Watson had been a possibility until the MPs had had to go pick him up from San Diego PD after he'd gotten into a drunken brawl with a Marine down from Pendleton. And worse, had lost.

The bottom line was, and had been then, that he'd never done it because there hadn't been anyone, of all the men he'd known, that he'd thought good enough or trustworthy enough for sweet, innocent Cara Thorpe.

Inwardly rattled, he stared down into his cup of coffee. If he'd felt that way when she'd been a shy, withdrawn girl, how did he feel now about the vibrant, confident woman across from him?

"How did you do it?" he asked, wondering, as soon as the words were out, what the hell had happened to his usual caution in speaking his thoughts out loud.

She blinked. "Do what?"

"Change so much."

She smiled, and he thought he saw a touch of ruefulness in it. Her words proved him right. "You mean from the little shrinking violet I used to be?"

"Well…yeah," he said, feeling awkward all over again, but curious enough to ignore it.

"Hope," she said simply. "I wanted to be like her. And after she…was gone, it seemed even more as if I should."

He noted the hesitation, knew from it that she, too, had faced too often that confusion over what to say, how to characterize Hope's absence. He'd never, even when his brain told him with cool logic that it was true, been able to call her dead. Not without knowing for sure. And he'd often chosen the word Cara had used. *Gone.* It was as good as anything under the circumstances.

But that wasn't what had really caught his attention. "As if you should?" he asked.

She gave a one-shouldered shrug, accompanied by a self-dep-recating smile. "I know it sounds ridiculous, but I felt like the world was a duller, less colorful place without Hope in it. And since I was as close as she had to a sister, it was up to me to…make it up to the world for losing her." The shrug came again. "Like I said, grief does crazy things to you. Makes you do crazy things."

He looked at her intently then, pondering her words. He saw the changes not just in her looks, but in the steady regard she returned, holding his gaze levelly, and in the refusal to avoid his eyes, as she once had regularly.

"There's nothing crazy about it," he said after a moment, meaning it. "Hope loved you like that sister, and trying to be like her is one of the most…moving tributes you could ever give her."

She blushed. That, at least, hadn't changed. "Thank you."

"But you're not, you know."

The color faded from her cheeks. "I know that. I could never be what she was."

She stopped when he held up a hand. "Don't. That's not what I meant. I meant you're not Hope, no one could be. But you shouldn't be, either. You're yourself, Cara, and that's enough."

"It is, now," she said. "But I wouldn't have gotten to here if not for Hope."

He shook his head. "You probably don't believe this, but it always was enough. You just didn't know it."

She stared at him. "Gabriel Taggert, that is one of the nicest thing anyone's ever said to me."

If he blushed, he'd be doing it now. He was thankful he wasn't prone to it. Instead, he rubbed the back of his neck again, wishing that annoying itch would go away.

"For what it's worth," Cara said, looking past him toward the door to the café, "at the moment we *are* being watched."

His fingers stopped. For a moment he was disconcerted that she'd noticed his action and correctly guessed the reason for it, but what she'd said was more important.

"By?" he asked, without looking around.

"There's a young woman over there near the door," she said, "talking to Mr. Woodruff, who must be on his lunch break since he has a cup of coffee in his hand. And he just pointed our way."

"Mr. Woodruff," Gabe said dryly, "appears to be local information central as well as gossip."

"Indeed."

She looked down as she dipped a French fry—some of the best he'd ever tasted and so probably fried in something artery-clogging—into a small pool of ketchup on her plate. She didn't wolf them down, he'd noticed, but savored each one with an enjoyment he himself hadn't applied to food in a long while. Then she looked over his shoulder again.

"Perhaps it was just coincidence," she said. "They're both gone from the doorway now, and I don't see her sitting anywhere."

"Or it wasn't us Woodruff was pointing at."

She nodded. "Possibly. Sure looked that way, though."

"Maybe we'll come across her when we start in on our canvass again. Would you recognize her?"

"Yes," Cara said. "She looked young, twenties. Very long, straight, dark hair. And she was thin, kind of angular. She looked…."

"What?"

Cara shrugged. "Just an impression. She seemed kind of… hyper. Her gestures were very quick, sharp."

"Interesting," Gabe said. Cara wasn't sure if he meant it, or if he was humoring her.

"I know it sounds silly to say, having only seen her from this distance, but—"

"It sounds observant," Gabe said.

She blinked. She hadn't expected that. "Well, I did get very good at that when I was younger."

"I noticed," Gabe said. "You were always watching people."

"You have time to do that when you don't talk much," she said wryly.

"I remember," Gabe said, "when you did talk what you said was generally well worth hearing."

"I…thank you."

"And you were right on about people. You knew Hope's supposed friend Jackie Carter was a phony the moment you saw her, even though Hope insisted she wasn't that bad."

"That's because she called me Hope's charity case, behind her back."

Gabe looked flatteringly offended. "You were never that. You should have told me. I would have dealt with her."

The thought of Gabriel Taggert leaping to her defense took her breath away. She scrambled to keep that image under wraps.

"Hope tended to see people the way she wanted them to be, not the way they were."

He lifted a brow at her. "Including me?"

She flushed, and for a moment she was that shy, quiet girl again, face-to-face with the man she'd fantasized about, terrified that somehow he might look at her and guess, and she'd be humiliated beyond belief. She fought down the old feelings, wondering if she'd ever be truly free of them, of that instinct to hide, to not draw attention, to stay safely hidden away and unnoticed.

"It might explain," he said casually, as if he hadn't noticed her reaction, "why she didn't deal with the reality of my life very well."

"Hope," she said, her voice a bit sharp with lingering embarrassment, "didn't deal with the reality well because she was more than a little spoiled. Her reaction to your career, and what it entailed, was typical."

He looked startled at her assessment. "Typical?"

"Hope's world centered around Hope. But she was so sweet and charming, most of us forgave her for it."

Gabe stared at her. "You certainly aren't the girl who thought she walked on water anymore, are you?"

The words stung a little, given the reason they were even together, but Cara had come a long way from that girl, and hiding her thoughts wasn't the way she dealt with things any longer.

"I love her like a sister, but like a sister, I'm not blind about her, either. There were things about her I didn't love. She wasn't perfect. And what happened to her doesn't make her perfect."

Gabe gave her a smile that told her he'd been down that road. "Hard to convince some people of that."

"It's human nature, when someone—"

When she stopped suddenly, Gabe's smile faded. "Dies," he said flatly. "That's what this is all about, isn't it? Proving that?"

"Yes," she said, admitting it aloud for the first time. "That's why it's hard to say anything…unflattering about her."

"I know." He stared down into his half-empty coffee cup.

"Let's just leave it at the fact that we both loved her. And we need to know what happened to her."

"Yes," she said quickly, thankful for his words. But she also felt the need to elaborate on what he'd said before. "But I haven't been that girl who worshiped Hope, not really, since she started giving you so much grief. You were honest with her. She knew what she was getting into when she married a naval officer, and she had no right to complain she hadn't."

"I did tell her it wouldn't be easy," he said.

"I know. So did I. But she loved you so much...I understood why she went ahead."

Cara lowered her gaze to her nearly empty plate then, afraid she'd gone too far this time, that he would read in her eyes the real reason she understood exactly why Hope had wanted to marry her dashing officer.

"Hope just didn't have the resources to deal with being alone," she said hastily, anything to keep him from seeing the truth. "She needed people around her to charm."

"She needed her husband around," Gabe said.

His tone was so flat Cara's gaze shot to his face. And for the first time she saw a trace of bitterness there, and more than a little self-blame.

"It wasn't your fault," she said quickly. "Hope couldn't grasp the concept of something bigger than herself, something that's worth sacrificing for. In that way, she was... shallow, I guess."

His expression changed then, became thoughtful, considering. "But you grasp it, don't you?"

"Yes," she said simply. "I'm just sorry others got in the way of it, for you."

It took a moment, but the smile that eventually curved his mouth was the most wonderful thing she'd ever seen. It was genuine, real, and went all the way to his eyes. He opened his mouth to speak, and she held her breath, thinking that if whatever he said matched that smile, she was going to be—

His gaze shifted as something caught his attention through the café window. His eyes narrowed, and he frowned.

"Long, straight, dark hair, you said?"

It took her a second to make the shift. "The woman? Yes. In a braid. Why?"

"She's across the street trying to get into my car."

Chapter 9

The woman took off the moment she spotted them coming out of the café. Gabe ran for the street, but she darted into an alley. By the time he'd dodged an oncoming lumber truck, she was out of sight. He raced toward where she'd disappeared, but stopped in his tracks when he reached the end of the short, narrow alley and there was no sign of her.

The alley wasn't wide enough for a car, and he hadn't heard one start anyway. It was more of a gap between buildings, and it opened onto another street at the other end. She could have gone either direction after that. Or into any of the buildings. If she was a local, she probably knew all the places to go if she didn't want to be seen.

He was standing in the alley, looking around in frustration when Cara caught up with him.

"It doesn't look like she got into the car," she said.

"That'll teach me to use the alarm, even up here," he muttered almost to himself, although he doubted he could ever get into the habit as the thing going off for no real reason annoyed him so much. He scanned the empty alley once more. "I wonder what she was after."

"I suppose it's too much to think she just wanted to look at the fancy car," Cara said.

Her tone was so glum Gabe knew she didn't believe it. It also told him she knew as well as he did that this was a development neither of them had expected.

"Especially after she apparently asked the helpful Mr. Woodruff about us."

"Maybe she just asked who owned the car in front of his post office," Cara suggested. "You can't tell me one of those babies shows up here every day."

"Maybe," he said, but he didn't quite believe it. "Sexist of me, I suppose, but I'd be more likely to believe that if it were a guy."

"Hey," she said in mock offense, "I'd stop and look at it, and I'm not a guy."

"Well, I am, so believe me, I noticed that."

She didn't answer, and he wondered if it was because his voice had sounded as grim as he thought it had. He didn't dare look at her, but with that peripheral vision of his, he saw she was looking at him rather oddly.

"Cara—"

"Shall we start on the other side of the street now? Or do you want to look for her?" Her tone was brisk, businesslike as she gestured down the alley.

Nice work, Taggert, he told himself. *You compliment her, but you sound like a growling bear doing it.* At least, he'd meant it as a compliment. But it had come out sounding like a warning.

And apparently she'd taken it that way.

Or had it been more of a warning to himself? Here they were, trying to track down what might be the only clue they'd ever really found to his wife's fate, and he was noticing another woman?

But it wasn't another woman. It was Cara.

His wife's best friend.

What that made all this, and the fact that he'd meant to compliment her at all, he couldn't begin to figure out right now.

Task at hand, Taggert, he told himself. *Focus.*

"Let's finish what we were doing," he said, striving for a normal tone of voice this time. "Maybe we'll come across her."

"And we can ask about her, too. Somebody's bound to know who she is."

Gabe nodded, grateful she didn't seem to be holding his gruffness against him. They started where they'd left off for lunch, working their way down the single main street. They'd fallen into a routine of Cara speaking to the women, Gabe to the men, because they'd found it more efficient. Cara said it was because it took the male-female thing out of the equation, and she didn't seem bothered by it at all.

Gabe thought it was simply that no man could resist flirting with a woman like Cara, and that would cut down the ease of the process.

He still marveled at the change in her. She'd become a very self-sufficient, confident woman, in addition to having left her quiet, plain appearance behind.

He thought suddenly of what she'd said just before he'd spotted the woman at his car.

Hope just didn't have the resources to deal with being alone....

Cara had loved Hope, but clearly she hadn't had blinders on. And for all his understanding of what it took to be a military spouse, he realized he'd never really accepted that Hope simply hadn't been cut out to be one. That it hadn't been anybody's fault, really; it just wasn't who she was. Some of the old, familiar ache he'd been carrying around seemed to ease, and he glanced at Cara in wonder that in a few hours she'd managed to clear up something he'd been trying to understand for years now.

Hope couldn't grasp the concept of something bigger than herself, something that's worth sacrificing for.

Her words echoed in his head again. She'd spoken them with a conviction that told him she meant what she'd said. Cara Thorpe, he thought, would have what it took. In her quiet way, she was stronger than Hope had ever been. All Hope's verve and energy had sprung not from strength but from a need he hadn't understood until it was too late.

"—trouble, that Crystal. Nothing but trouble."

Gabe focused suddenly on the conversation going on at his elbow. He'd almost tuned out when it was clear the woman working behind the counter of the small, tourist-trap–style gift shop had been there only three years, so hadn't been there when Hope had been in town.

But apparently Cara had asked about the woman who had tried to get into his car.

"Trouble?" Cara's gaze flicked to Gabe, then back to the grandmotherly woman she'd been speaking to. "What kind of trouble?"

"You name it, that girl's been into it. Ungrateful, too. She'd be in jail, I'm sure, if people weren't so tolerant around here. Or if she were a better thief."

"So…we were right to be concerned when she tried the door of the car?"

The woman's brows lifted. "She try to steal something from you, too? Can't believe she still shows her face in town, she should be so ashamed."

"Do you know where she lives now?" Gabe asked.

The woman gave him a careful look, having to tilt her head back slightly to see his face. Finally she answered. "Last I heard, she was living at the old inn, on Big Tree Road."

"Inn?"

"A couple of miles out of town. Used to be a fancy sort of place, somebody had an idea we'd be the next Aspen or something. Rose Terhune bought it ten years ago, although what a single woman needs with that much space I'll never know. But she's sort of an odd duck anyway. Those artist and writer types usually are. But to let that girl stay there rent free, when all she does is cause problems…."

It took a few minutes for Cara to extricate them from the woman's righteous indignation, but finally they were back outside.

"Well," Cara said, "wasn't that interesting?"

"Interesting," Gabe agreed, "but I don't know how helpful."

"Thinking now she might just have been trying to steal something out of an obviously expensive car?"

"Maybe," he said, having to admit the possibility had become more probable after the character assessment they'd just gotten. "But out there on the main street, with witnesses all around?"

Cara rubbed her arms as they stood pondering their next stop. It had clouded over, and there was a crispness in the air that hadn't been there when they'd arrived earlier that afternoon. Even he, who had a pretty wide comfort zone, felt a little chilly.

"Let's go back to the car for jackets," he said.

"Kind of you to notice," Cara said.

For a moment he thought it was a jab, that maybe she'd been cold for some time and he hadn't realized it, but there was no undertone to her voice and nothing but sincerity in her face as she looked up at him.

"Gabe?"

He realized he'd been staring at her; he didn't know for how long. He snapped out of it with a start and a mental chiding; he didn't understand why he was having so much trouble focusing on the task at hand, something he usually excelled at.

"Sorry," he muttered. "Let's go."

When they got back to the car he opened it, reached in and grabbed the fleece jacket he'd given her back at the boat. He held it for her as she slipped her arms into the sleeves. She pulled it close around her gratefully, and thanked him for the small courtesy with no sign of offense. It was clearly too big for her, but she snuggled into it as if grateful for the warmth.

She'd let him open doors for her, too, he thought. But then, just as often she opened them for others in the same way, so he put that down to basic good manners. His mother had been big on that, and it was a lesson pounded into him from an early age. For her, as for his father, the phrase "an officer and a gentleman" had had true resonance. He kept up the practice now in her memory, even if it earned him puzzled looks or teasing, and the occasional snide remark.

They had about a quarter of the main street left to go. Gabe was beginning to doubt they would find out anything useful, but it simply wasn't in him to leave the job three-quarters done. He suspected Cara would feel the same way.

But if he was right, and they finished the task they'd set and found nothing, then what? Give up and go home, after a simple if lengthy walk down the single main street of the town Hope had visited on the last day anyone had seen her?

"You're frowning."

He blinked. "Sorry. Thinking."

"About Hope." It wasn't a question, but an assumption.

"In a way," he said. "But more about what happens if we don't find anything down there." He gestured toward the portion of the street they hadn't covered yet as they started walking that way.

"I've been thinking about that," Cara said. "I want to look around more, off the main drag, see if maybe I can find someone who knows who Miriam is."

He nodded in agreement. "She's the key."

"I took a couple of vacation days to deal with this, but I realize you probably need to get back to work," she said. "So I can just come back in my own car tomorrow."

"Actually, I was thinking of staying, if that little motel has room."

She looked relieved. "If I could have figured out a way to get home tomorrow, that would have been my first choice. You're sure you can be away? On no notice?"

"One thing about Redstone, if you need personal time, you get it."

"Just like that?"

"Josh makes it so easy that nobody much abuses it."

She looked thoughtful. "I think that says as much about the caliber of people he hires as anything."

"Perhaps. He doesn't often hire bad apples. And when they do turn up, they're dealt with in short order. Josh is an amazingly generous boss, but he won't be taken advantage of. Not for long, anyway."

"I'd like to meet him someday."

"You'd like him." He stopped walking as they neared the general store where Mr. Woodruff reigned. "And he'd like you. And what you've accomplished."

She grinned suddenly. "Maybe I could interest him in a new Web site."

He smiled back at her, but that grin had taken the breath right out of him. Somehow he managed to say, "Maybe you could," before they went inside to purchase what they would need for an overnight stay.

"Call me fussy," Cara said, "but brushing my teeth is a requirement."

"Me, too," Gabe said with a laugh. They split up inside and found that the little store, amazingly, held all the basics they'd hoped for. They dropped the bags off at his car—with Gabe setting the alarm this time—then resumed their original quest.

They stopped in front of a chalet-style building that, according to the sign in front, housed the chamber of commerce, the community center and the library. It was the latter that was their goal; Hope had been a fairly voracious reader, and she loved libraries.

The librarian startled them. At first glance Gabe would have put him at maybe eighteen, but the freshly minted college degree on the wall behind the checkout counter that was crammed into one corner of the larger of the two rooms that made up the library told him the kid had to be at least twenty-two. Unless he was a child prodigy of some sort. Which seemed possible; under a mop of hair almost the same color as Cara's, intelligent and lively eyes looked back at him.

And looked at Cara with an appreciation that made age irrelevant.

"Hi, I'm Greg Mercer. Before you ask, yes I'm really the librarian, and yes, I'm old enough."

He said it with such a wide grin Gabe knew he'd heard the

inevitable questions often. That he'd decided to handle them with humor was something Gabe respected.

"So how'd it happen?" Cara asked with a laugh that made the young man's grin widen.

"Harry Potter," he said succinctly.

"Never underestimate the power of a good book," Cara said, earning another grin.

"Especially at a very impressionable age," he said. He glanced at Gabe, then back to her. "So what can I help you with?"

"Unless you were working here eight years ago, I'm not sure you can," Gabe said dryly, annoyed with himself for finding the instant rapport Cara seemed to develop with the young man irritating.

"Obviously I wasn't," Greg said. "But I did practically live here. I've got three younger siblings, and this was the only place where I could read in peace."

"You grew up here in Pine Lake?" Cara asked.

Grew up? Gabe thought. *Still waiting on that.*

Greg nodded. "And came back after college, amazingly enough. But I had a built-in job. Mrs. Barker, the old librarian, promised me I'd get it when she retired, if I wanted it. She even held off retiring until I was done with school." He gestured at his small domain. "It's not big, and it doesn't pay a lot, but it's a start."

Cara took out the photograph. "Do you happen to recognize her?"

The boy's eyes widened. "Er…yeah, I do. I mean, I don't know her, but I remember seeing her."

"You're sure?" Gabe asked. "It would have been a long time ago."

"I know it was. But it's not as if a geeky kid like I was would forget seeing a woman like that in the little old Pine Lake library."

"She was in here?" Gabe's voice sharpened. He couldn't help it.

"I think I remember seeing her a couple of times. I hung out in the kid's section—" he gestured toward the secondary, smaller room at the back "—mostly, but she came in there once. Looking at picture books."

"Laura's baby," Cara murmured.

"Did you ever talk to her?"

"Me?" He looked startled. "Never. I was just a stupid kid, she was this gorgeous, totally hot woman. I thought she'd crush me like a bug if I tried to talk to her."

While Gabe wrestled with the image of a young teenager with hormones running amok ogling his wife, Cara smiled at the young man.

"She wouldn't have," Cara said. "She would have been very nice. And," she added, "I doubt you were ever stupid."

He was still young enough to blush. And Gabe felt like a cranky old man for his reaction to the kid. How had he gotten to feeling this way, so old at thirty-eight?

"The old librarian," he began, making sure his voice was level.

"Mrs. Barker? She was nice. Let me hang out even after hours while she closed up sometimes, as long as I was reading."

"Does she still live here?"

The young man shook his head sadly. "No. She died last year. Right after she retired. I'm telling you, don't ever retire, it'll kill you."

"I'm sorry," Cara said.

"Me, too. She was okay. She was the first person I ever knew, I mean really knew, who died."

Okay, so that's why I feel so old around him, Gabe thought. I *am.*

"That's always hard," Cara said sympathetically. "It's always a shock to find out…what forever really means."

Young Greg blinked. "Yes. That's it, exactly."

With that possible trail gone, Gabe thought it was time they moved on. It was Cara who asked about Miriam. Gabe hadn't even been going to bring it up, but the moment she did he realized he should have thought less about the boy's age and more about the fact that he'd grown up here in Pine Lake.

"You mean Miriam Hammon, our most famous resident?"

Cara drew back slightly, clearly as startled as he was. If she was so famous, why was this the first person they'd found who'd ever heard of her?

"Famous?" Cara said tentatively.

"Well, she was. She's not working anymore, at least not writing. I think she's painting now."

"She's a writer?"

"She was. Fairly successful in her day. I remember Mrs. Barker was all excited when she moved up here. I looked at her books, because I thought I wanted to be a writer, but there were no magic or wizards, so I didn't care, then."

Cara lifted a brow at the last word. "And now?"

"I've read them. Woman's stuff, mostly, but I need to know about that, too. She really was good. Too bad she's not writing anymore."

"Is that why no one else in town seems to know who she is?" Gabe asked.

Greg's brow furrowed. "Everybody knows about her."

Gabe's gaze narrowed. "Then why did everyone we asked say they'd never heard the name?"

The young man's expression cleared. "Oh. That's it. She didn't write under her real name. She wrote as Rose Terhune."

Gabe went still. Cara glanced at him. Hope's friend was the woman who had given refuge to the troublesome woman who had tried to break into his car?

All of a sudden things had gotten complicated.

Chapter 10

"That has to be the place," Gabe said.

"Yes," Cara agreed. "It looks like it could easily have been a small inn, once."

The big house, which sat amid a cluster of small buildings that looked as if they could have been guest cottages once, looked expansive and inviting. It seemed a bit out of place among the more rustic and cabinlike structures they'd passed, most of them finished in natural woods, some of them with A-line roofs that gave them that mountain feel. This place had a steep roof—for snow, she guessed, although as a Southern California girl through and through she'd never seen much of the stuff—but was painted a soft yellow with bright white trim. It stood out among its camouflaged neighbors, but not in a bad way. It looked….

"Cheerful," she said.

"I guess," Gabe said neutrally.

She squelched a smile; Gabe had always had a typically male wariness about assigning emotions to color. In fact, he'd had a certain wariness about color, period. Once, on a rare occasion when she'd felt brave enough, she'd asked him teasingly if the navy had regulations that applied to his civilian clothes as well, if that was why he rarely wore anything other than grays, blacks, or blues. Hope, whose own favorite color was a vivid purple, had joined in. Shortly thereafter Hope had bought him a shirt in that shade. Cara had guessed he only wore it to please Hope, and please her it had.

And any other female who saw him in it, Cara remembered. The color had set off his dark hair and tanned skin in a way that caught the eye of any woman in the vicinity who was still breathing.

"Quite a garden," Gabe said.

"Glorious," Cara said, "even though it's not in full bloom yet."

"Good planning," Gabe said. "Things that are interesting even in winter."

That, too, was very Gabe, she thought. He appreciated the bones of things, the design, the foundation that made them work. She supposed it was part of what had made him like the navy; he'd known his ship from the keel up, the design, all the systems, everything that made it work.

They followed the pleasantly curved pathway through the garden. Cara saw shady places where there was snow still on the ground, but spring was beginning to win the yearly battle. The walk was intriguing, with new sights at each turn, a shrub with striking red stems here, a pyramidal trellis there, and a bed of brightly purple crocuses still hanging on to blooms there. Other plants were budding madly, and Cara imagined that in just another month the place would be in furious growth, and in two months would be spectacular.

"A lot of work goes into creating this kind of random effect," she mused aloud.

Gabe looked at her sharply. "I was just thinking that. That for all the casual effect, this was very carefully planned."

His surprise that they'd had the same thought made her smile. "I wonder if it was already here, or if it's our writer?"

"Let's ask," Gabe said, and only then did Cara realize he was looking past her, toward the house.

She turned. The woman approaching them, a questioning but not unfriendly expression on her face, looked to be in her forties, although from glancing through the books Greg had shown them, Cara was sure she must be older. She was about Cara's height and had that trim, wiry appearance that promised she would probably look much the same into her seventies.

She was wearing a crisp, long-sleeved white blouse tucked into faded but clean jeans, and a leather belt with what looked like real silver conchos threaded through the belt loops. Her hair was cut short and liberally streaked with gray amid the darker strands. She seemed utterly unselfconscious about it, and that coupled with her relatively unlined face made her seem much more youthful than the gray suggested.

"Hello," she said. "Can I help you?"

Her voice was pleasant, even welcoming. Cara had been so distracted by the enchanting garden she hadn't really thought about how to approach this.

"We were admiring your garden," she said, while she tried to decide how to bring up Hope. "It's beautiful even now, and it must be amazing later in the spring."

The woman's golden brown eyes lit up. "It is. I'm very proud of it."

"I can't imagine how much work it must be, to keep it from going crazy," Cara said, smiling as she waved at the profuse plantings.

"It is that," the woman said. "I had to bring in some help, or I'd never be able to keep up with it and my work, too."

So was she still writing after all? Cara wondered. "You work here, at home?" she asked, still unsure of what approach to take with this alert-eyed, kindly seeming woman.

"Yes, I do. I paint."

Greg had said that, Cara recalled. "You certainly have a lot of subject matter," she said, glancing around. "Your garden, the mountains, the trees…" She stopped suddenly, then couldn't help laughing at herself. "Assuming that's what you paint, of course. Which I shouldn't have done."

The woman responded with a smiling laugh of her own. "I'm very much a beginner at this, so I wouldn't dare claim to paint anything anyone might expect to recognize."

Even Gabe chuckled at that.

"I'm Cara Thorpe," she said, holding out her hand.

The woman took it. Her grip was definite, but not forceful. "Miriam Hammon." As she said it she was frowning, not in anger but as if she were puzzled. "Cara Thorpe," she repeated.

"Yes. I'm a friend of—"

"Hope!" the woman exclaimed suddenly, smiling widely.

"Yes," Cara said, relieved.

Miriam's gaze shot to Gabe. "Gabe Taggert," he said.

Miriam's smile widened even farther. "I wondered if that was you! You don't look much different than in the photograph Hope showed me. Tall, dark and handsome, she used to say."

Gabe shifted his feet as if he were uncomfortable. Cara felt the urge to laugh at his discomfiture. Didn't the man have a mirror? she wondered.

But the urge vanished at Miriam Hammon's next words. "It's been so long. How is Hope? I hope she's well, I've missed her visits."

Cara opened her mouth, but no words came. After a moment of silence that brought a frown to Miriam's face, Gabe said quietly, "We were hoping you could tell us."

The woman drew back slightly, obviously puzzled. "Me? But I haven't seen her for…oh, several years now."

"Eight?" Gabe suggested.

"I suppose it could have been that long. I'd have to check. But…what are you saying? That *you* don't know where she is?"

Cara finally found her tongue. "She went missing eight years ago."

Miriam gasped. "Missing?"

"No one's seen or heard from her since," Gabe said.

"My word," Miriam said, her hand going to her throat as if she were having trouble taking in enough air. Cara knew the feeling.

"But we've recently discovered she was here in Pine Lake on the day she disappeared," she said.

"You'd both better come inside," Miriam said. "I'll put coffee on."

She led them, not to the big front entrance, but to a smaller doorway that led directly into a large, country-style kitchen.

"I'm afraid what used to be the lobby is now my studio," she explained. "It has the best light."

The kitchen was warm and welcoming, in the same yellow and white color scheme as the exterior of the house, with touches of a deep green that echoed the fir trees outside. Copper pots and pans hung from a rack over a large, commercial-style range with six burners and a grill in between them.

"Lovely," she said, looking around as Miriam gestured them to two of the stools pulled up to a huge island topped with a granite slab that was polished to a high sheen.

"This was a bed-and-breakfast place before I bought it," Miriam explained as she scooped coffee into a filter and put it into a coffee maker that sat next to the big, stainless-steel refrigerator. "A bit bigger than most, with space for a dozen guests, and they fixed breakfast in here."

"Good space," Gabe said.

He could, Cara noted, easily reach the hanging pans she'd have to stretch for. As would Miriam, she thought.

"Too bad it's wasted on me," Miriam said with a quick smile that Cara thought charming. "I'm not much of a cook."

She got three mugs from the cupboard above the coffeemaker. They were utilitarian, heavy stoneware, but each was painted with a different design in the same deep green on white, making them clearly part of a set yet not numbingly the same. The very kind of thing that would appeal to Hope, Cara thought.

"Did you paint these?" Cara asked.

"Why, yes, I did," Miriam said.

"I like them."

"Thank you, dear. I've always dabbled, but only lately did I realize that the time was now or never, if I wanted to truly learn to paint."

"So you quit writing?" Gabe asked.

"Oh, no. I will always write. I write for myself, and short stories occasionally, and I'm working at my own pace on a children's book. But I put an end to the book-a-year grind about three years ago, yes."

When the coffeepot was full, she filled all three mugs, slid a container of sugar across the counter to them, and got a carton of milk out of the refrigerator.

She sat down herself as she poured a dollop of milk into her own mug.

"Now, let's get to it," she said briskly. "What on earth happened?"

"I wish we knew," Cara said. "May I ask how you and Hope met?"

"She wrote me a fan letter." The woman's golden eyes flicked to Gabe. "After a book I wrote that featured a woman married to a military officer. It was a lovely letter, but it was also filled with such anxiety that I urged her to get help. To contact Family Services at the naval base. I knew from my research that there were resources available to her."

"I told her the same thing," Gabe said, an echo of frustration in his voice. It was tinged with a note of despair that dug at Cara's heart. "But she never did it. I asked one of the fleet and Family Services counselors to contact her periodically, to make sure she was all right. She wouldn't even talk to him."

"She told me she felt she didn't fit in with the other families, the other wives," Miriam said.

"Hope wasn't much for fitting into a group," Cara said, still disturbed by how Gabe had sounded, as if this were all somehow his fault. "She was used to being the star."

"She had that quality," Miriam agreed. "Everyone was drawn to her, to her beauty, her charm. In any case, she wrote to me again, thanking me for my concern. After my next book was released, she wrote again, via e-mail, and we began to correspond regularly."

Miriam's expression changed, became thoughtful. "Excuse me a moment, please. I want to check on something on my computer."

Cara looked at Gabe as the woman left the room. "You had no idea about this?"

"None," Gabe said grimly.

"Neither did I. Not that she had to tell me everything, but…."

"She always did."

"I thought so, yes," Cara admitted. "We shared so much. I thought we knew everything about each other."

"So did I," he said. "Obviously I was wrong."

She reached out and laid a hand over his on the granite counter. "Maybe she would have, eventually. Maybe she just didn't want to take up the precious time you had together talking about other things."

"Something important enough for her to make the trip up here so often? You don't think she should have told me about that?"

"Should have? Of course." Cara lowered her gaze. "But then, Hope always did say I had some funny ideas about relationships."

"Funny? To tell your spouse the truth?"

"She didn't lie," Cara said, feeling stirred to defend her dearest friend. "She just didn't share this part of her life. Maybe there was a reason."

"Yes," Gabe said, sounding grim. "Maybe there was."

Chapter 11

Miriam came back moments later, interrupting what had threatened to become a difficult conversation. Gabe kept thinking of what Cara had said, that maybe Hope had had a reason for keeping this from him. None of the reasons he could come up with were particularly pleasant.

"I remembered what I was working on the last time I saw Hope," Miriam said, thankfully derailing his tangled thoughts. "She had dropped in unexpectedly, as she often did, and I let her read the opening chapter of the book I'd just started. I just pulled up the copy I archived, and it says the file was created just over eight years ago."

"Over?" Gabe asked.

"By about three months."

"How long had she been coming here, by then?"

"A couple of years, I think. We met when she came to a book signing. Her visits here began after that."

Gabe went still. "Wait. She told me about that. That she'd gotten a book autographed by her favorite writer."

So Hope hadn't kept everything a secret, he thought.

"But she was here after that," Cara said. "She mailed a postcard from here almost exactly eight years ago."

Miriam shook her head. "I didn't see her. I remember because she said she was going to come back every month, to read what I'd written. She wanted to follow the entire process. But she never did."

Gabe felt his jaw clench as he struggled to wrap his mind around this side of his wife he'd known nothing about.

"Why?" he asked. "I don't mean to be insulting, and I can understand anyone's interest in knowing a real writer, but—"

Miriam studied him for a moment. "You didn't know, did you?"

"Apparently there's a lot I didn't know," Gabe said, his voice tight again.

"It must have been hard, you being away so much," Miriam said. "I told her she should talk to you about it. About her dream."

Gabe was about at the end of his patience. Cara seemed to sense that. "Dream?" she asked.

"After we'd corresponded for some time, and she'd made a couple of visits up here, she confided that she'd been thinking she would like to try writing."

Gabe went still. "She what?"

"She said she'd always kept journals, which is not a bad first step. And her letters, and later e-mails, were always very readable and as vivid and vivacious as she herself was. So I saw no reason to discourage her. I thought there might be potential there."

"Hope wanted to be a writer?"

Gabe knew he sounded astonished. Only the fact that Cara looked as if she were barely keeping herself from echoing his words eased his discomfiture; how had he not known this?

"She didn't know what she wanted to write," Miriam answered, "but yes. I suggested, given the nature of her letters, that she try feature articles, perhaps starting out on Web site publications, then on to magazines or newspapers."

Gabe let out a compressed breath. Cara was shaking her head.

"I gather neither of you knew this?" Miriam asked gently.

"No," Cara said. "And we should have."

"Sometimes," Miriam said, "when people have a dream they think will never come true, they keep it hidden, for fear of being thought foolish."

"And Hope would hate looking foolish," Cara said.

Gabe's gut knotted. Had he been so judgmental that his wife couldn't even share a dream like this with him? Had she thought he would laugh, or in fact consider it foolish?

Would he have?

He didn't think so. He wanted to think he would have supported her wholeheartedly, but that was easy to think now, driven by guilt.

Miriam studied them both for a moment. "Perhaps it's the writer in me, but I can't help noticing…you're both using a combination of past and present tense."

"A battle I've been fighting for eight years," Gabe said, suddenly feeling utterly weary.

"So it's true, she simply…vanished?"

Gabe said, "She's never been found."

Miriam looked up at him at that. "Is there a difference?"

"Yes." It nearly burst from him, with a sense of urgency he couldn't seem to keep under wraps.

"Of course there is," Cara said. "Especially to a logical mind. Vanished is…inexplicable. Mysterious."

Gabe drew back slightly in surprise. He hadn't expected her to understand that. It made it easier to go on more calmly.

"No one just vanishes. There's an explanation, always. It may never be found by those left behind, but that doesn't mean it isn't there."

"A logical mind," Miriam echoed with a knowing expression that made Gabe wonder just what Hope had told her about him.

"Didn't you wonder, when you didn't hear from her?" Cara asked.

Miriam nodded. "Of course. I kept e-mailing her for some time, after she quit coming. She never answered. I always thought that she'd simply changed her mind about writing. I never lied to her about the difficulties of achieving success, or keeping it once you got there."

"Reality again," Cara murmured, then winced.

The knot in his Gabe's eased a little as he read the meaning behind Cara's quiet words and her own reaction to them. *Another dream world destroyed for Hope by reality?* he guessed she had thought. Followed quickly by guilt as her conscience told her she shouldn't be thinking that way about Hope, not now. It was a process he himself was far too familiar with.

"Then I wondered," Miriam went on with a look at Gabe, "if something had happened to you. She was always afraid of that."

Gabe drew back slightly. "She was?"

"Of course she was. Given your work, how could she not be?"

"We all were," Cara put in. "No matter how many times you told us you were perfectly safe."

"She never said a word," Gabe said, sounding a bit lame even to his own ears. Cara looked as if she were going to laugh, in spite of everything. "Neither did you," he felt compelled to point out.

"It hardly seemed necessary to dwell on the obvious."

"Men," Miriam said with a shake of her head.

Cara did laugh then. Gabe shifted uncomfortably; the looks the two women exchanged made it clear that any woman would understand the layers of that simple exclamation.

And then Cara reached into her purse and pulled out the postcard. She handed it to the older woman.

"She had tried to call me that morning," Cara explained, "but I wasn't there. I called her back when I got the message, but it went straight to her voice mail."

Gabe stifled a twinge at the mention of Hope's voice mail. He'd checked it periodically, hoping to find something, anything, that would help, until the number was finally unavailable. Cara, he'd found, had called many times. He'd wondered if she did it just to hear her friend's voice on the cheery greeting. He'd found it nearly unbearable, after a while, but Cara had kept on.

Miriam read the message on the card and smiled. "It's very much Hope, isn't it?"

"Yes."

The woman looked at the card a moment longer, then her brows furrowed. "But if you had this, then you knew she'd been here at least once."

She'd been quick to pick up on that, Gabe thought.

"That's just it. I didn't have it," Cara said. "It was just delivered to me yesterday."

"Yesterday?"

Miriam looked at the card again to confirm the date on the postmark, just as he had done, as Hope's parents had done, as Cara herself had no doubt done.

"It came sealed in an envelope from the post office, with a letter of apology. I had moved, and somehow the forwarding order didn't work on everything, and only when I moved again and put in a second one, did this catch up with me."

Miriam's eyes widened as she looked up from the card to Cara. "So you've heard nothing for all those years, and then out of the blue this arrives?"

Cara nodded.

"That must have stopped your heart for a moment," Miriam said, reaching out to put a hand over Cara's where it rested on the granite countertop. The gesture was simple, comforting, and gave Gabe a clue to what Hope had found here with this kind, intelligent woman.

"And as for you," Miriam said, looking at Gabe thoughtfully, "I'd wager you're not at all sure how to feel."

"I haven't been," Gabe admitted, unable to dissemble at the moment, "for eight years."

Miriam shook her head. "This is a fresh shock for me, since I've just learned of it. But after all those years, you must have assumed she was dead."

"Eventually, it seemed the only conclusion, yes," Cara said, flicking a glance at Gabe.

Miriam looked at the card once more. "I don't understand. If she was here that day, why didn't she come to see me?"

"You weren't expecting her?" Gabe asked.

"No, but she often liked to surprise me and just pop in."

"That's quite a drive, if you happened not to be home."

"But I'm always home. Or not far away," she said. "I traveled the world for too many years, doing research, searching out new settings for books." A flicker of sadness crossed her face, and Gabe wondered what she had to regret about a life that many would covet. "I swore that someday I would settle in and stay put, and when I came here I did that. Hope knew that."

The woman's expression of sadness deepened then, she blinked rapidly for a moment, and Gabe guessed the reality of the news they'd brought was at last setting in.

"I shall miss her, tremendously. I never forgot her, even after all this time. I should have known she wouldn't simply forsake our relationship without a word like that."

"I'm sorry," Cara said, leaning forward and putting her hand over Miriam's in turn. "And thank you for being her...mentor."

"Mentor? I suppose I was. But she was just as important to me." Miriam looked at them both as if considering whether to go on. "I lost my only daughter to cancer twenty years ago. She was only sixteen. It destroyed my family. My husband left soon after. Hope...eased that pain. She was like Lorna in many ways, bright, beautiful...."

"I'm sorry," Gabe said.

A thud cut off whatever Miriam had been about to reply. The sound made them all turn toward the back door that had just slammed open against the wall.

Gabe sensed rather than saw Cara tense.

It was the woman with the braid who had tried to break into his car.

And she was glaring at them.

Chapter 12

"Ah, there you are," Miriam said. "This is Crystal Lowden. She helps out around here, with the house and the garden."

The young woman continued to glare at both her and Gabe. Angry, she thought. This was a very angry person.

"Come in," Miriam said. "Meet Cara Thorpe and Gabriel Taggert. My friend Hope's best friend and husband, respectively."

So she'd known Hope, Cara gathered from the form of the introduction. If she was right about her age, she would have been about sixteen when Hope was last here. She could—

"*That* one? Thought that was over and done," the girl said sharply, cutting off her speculation.

"Manners, Crystal," Miriam said without heat. "They're guests."

"Guests?" Crystal nearly snarled the words. "They staying?"

"We hadn't quite gotten to that point," Miriam said, apparently oblivious to the rudeness, "although I was about to make the offer, since it's getting late to be just starting the drive down the mountain."

She turned back to them. "Will you stay? I would love the chance to talk with you more, about Hope."

"We couldn't inconvenience you like that."

Cara's response was automatic and polite, but the moment she said it she sensed Gabe tense, and wondered if he wished she hadn't made it. Fortunately, Miriam didn't take the refusal easily.

"My dear, if you'll recall, this used to be an inn. Two people are not an imposition. Besides—" she lifted a hand to her eyes, wiped at them "—I've only just learned Hope is gone. I'd like to talk to the people closest to her."

"And I'd like to get to know you," Gabe said. Cara flicked a glance at him, wondering if he was silently adding *because I should have known all along*.

It wouldn't surprise her. He seemed determined to take so much of the blame on himself for Hope's disappearance, even for the state of their marriage before she'd gone. Maybe this would help him to learn more about the reason she'd left home that day, to know for sure that she hadn't intended never to return.

"Then it's settled," Miriam said, clearly genuinely pleased. "Crystal, will you get the blue and green rooms ready?" She looked back at them, ignoring the near-growl that emitted from the young woman's mouth. "Although if you prefer, you could have two of the cottages. Most I'm afraid I've taken over for storage, but there are a couple I keep clear for guests."

"Whatever works best for you," Cara said, and felt Gabe relax as he saw she wasn't going to resist staying here. She glanced up at his face, and saw something there that told her there was more to this than simply wanting to get to know someone who had clearly been important to Hope.

Her gaze flicked to Crystal, who looked mutinous as Miriam reconfirmed her first request.

"Those rooms, then, Crystal. Thank you, dear."

Miriam was as polite as the younger woman was rude. Crystal fiddled with something in the pocket of the denim bib overalls, what looked like the handles of a pair of garden clippers. For a moment Cara wondered if she'd refuse the request. But finally and without another word the woman turned and stalked out a different door, slamming it behind her even more loudly than she'd shoved the exterior door open. Cara couldn't help the expression of puzzlement that crossed her face.

"Don't mind her," Miriam said. "Crystal has had a very rough life, for all her youth."

"And how much of that has she brought on herself?" Gabe asked wryly as another slam echoed from somewhere else in the house.

Cara wondered if Miriam would take offense at the question she, too, had been thinking, but only he had the nerve to voice. The woman's smile told them she wasn't as unaware as she'd seemed.

"A lot," Miriam admitted. "She has a very difficult time trusting anyone or anything. I don't know her whole story, but what I do know is frighteningly ugly."

"We saw her, in town," Cara began.

Miriam sighed. "And heard about her, I'm sure."

"Yes," Gabe said.

"I know the reputation she has. And that most of Pine Lake thinks I'm crazy for letting her stay here."

Concern for this woman who apparently lived alone and had been important to Hope filled Cara. Did she really know Crystal's reputation, and choose to ignore it? Had the woman in the gift shop been right about Crystal's stealing?

"We saw her trying to get into Gabe's car," she said.

"Oh, no. She didn't take anything, did she?"

"She didn't actually get in," Gabe said.

Miriam frowned. "I'm very sorry. I thought she'd finally broken that habit."

"She has a habit of breaking into cars?" Gabe asked. His tone was mild, but Cara sensed he was suddenly fully alert. And she had a feeling it had little to do with the actual threat to his expensive car.

"No, but of trying. She used to survive on the streets that way, finding unlocked cars, pilfering small things she could use or sell for cash for food. But she doesn't take anything, not anymore. At least, she hasn't. I think she does it now just to…keep her skills sharp."

"Keep her skills sharp," Cara echoed, a little incredulous at the analogy.

Miriam nodded. "Some lessons, especially painful early ones, can't be unlearned. She expects to be back on the street at any moment. Even though she's been welcome here with me since she was sixteen."

Cara felt Gabe's tension go up another notch. She thought she knew why, certain he'd done the same math she had. Then he spoke softly and she knew she'd been right.

"While Hope was still coming here."

"Why, yes, they did meet, but only two or three times." Miriam smiled ruefully. "And Hope thought I was as crazy as you do, taking her on."

"You have a generous spirit," Cara said, all the while trying to figure out what this might mean in light of why they were here.

"Perhaps. My son says I'm trying to make up for losing Lorna by taking in strays."

Cara wasn't sure she didn't agree with that assessment. "Your son?"

"Lawrence. He lives down in San Bernardino." She shook her head. "He never understood my moving, either. That I wanted to get away from the place where Lorna had grown up. He got very upset when I mentioned selling the house, so I gave it to him when I moved up here."

"He and his sister were close?" Cara asked.

"Very." Her face changed then, took on an expression of sorrow so deep, so harsh, that for a moment she looked like a different woman, much older, much more worn and tired. "They were twins. Even though they obviously weren't identical, he was never the same after she died."

"Some wounds never really heal," Gabe said. "Nor should they."

A shiver went through Cara as she heard him speak in a quiet, soothing voice she hadn't heard since the time he'd comforted her when her favorite aunt had died the year before he and Hope had gotten married. It reminded her forcefully that there was another side to this man than the coolly analytical side, a side he didn't often show, but when he did, the effect was remarkable. There was something about such a strong man who could be so gentle that was incredibly moving.

She should have kept in touch after Hope disappeared, no matter what, she thought again. Neither of them should have had to go through that process alone, not when Hope was so dear to both of them. But her feelings for him had kept her from doing so, and she supposed she would always regret that.

Miriam was looking at Gabe with a new respect. "Thank you. You're exactly right. Some wounds shouldn't heal, not completely. What would it say about my love for my daughter if I simply got over losing her?"

Cara had never thought about it in quite that way, but she certainly couldn't argue the point.

"Now," Miriam said briskly, "you're welcome to dinner, but I tend to eat late. I usually don't even think about it, I'm afraid, until it's dark and I lose the light. Since sunset's at sevenish this time of year, it's usually eight or nine by the time I get around to actually eating."

Cara glanced at her watch. It was just after six, which startled her. The nearly four hours they'd been here had flown, it seemed.

"We actually just had a late lunch at about three," she told Miriam.

"Then nine should be about right for you," Miriam said, refusing to take the explanation as a decline of her offer. She seemed genuinely pleased at the prospect of their company. Cara looked at Gabe, who gave the slightest nod of his head; he wanted to stay. She understood. Of course he wanted to talk to this woman who, unbeknownst to him, had clearly been a big part of Hope's life.

"I warn you, however," Miriam added with a smile, "if you

want a decent meal you'll have to pitch in. I tend to throw together what's handy and quick."

Cara smiled. "I'll be happy to help."

"Why don't we go to the market and pick up some things?" Gabe suggested. "And we'll cook *you* dinner."

Miriam's smile became a grin. "And he cooks, too?"

Gabe shrugged, but Cara saw one corner of his mouth lift. "I've been known to, on occasion."

"I suppose it's rude to have your guests cook for you, but the thought of eating something I didn't have to fix myself and that didn't come out of a drive-through bag is far too tempting."

Cara grinned back at her. She *liked* this woman, and would have even if not for the connection to Hope. "It's not rude at all," she said. "We're taking up your time and space, it's only fair."

Miriam shook her head. "You're Hope's people. It's no trouble."

Cara noticed Gabe checking his car out before they got into it to head to the small grocery that Miriam had warned them closed at eight.

"Thinking Crystal was busy again?"

"Just checking," he said.

"Maybe the sight of this car was just too much temptation. I'd guess this would be a lush target, back in the days Miriam spoke of."

"Could be," he agreed.

"Which would mean," Cara said once they'd started down the narrow lane back to the main—which meant two narrow lanes—highway into town, "that it has nothing to do with why we're here."

"Not everything has to," he admitted. "That's the problem when you're so focused on a mission, you have to fight the tendency to assume everything that happens is somehow connected to it."

A mission. Cara pondered his choice of words. A holdover from his training, she supposed. Although she couldn't deny that the words fit; wasn't that exactly what they were on?

"What you said before, about some wounds shouldn't ever completely heal," she began.

Gabe glanced at her, but only for an instant; the narrow winding road required his attention. "What about it?"

"I never thought of it that way," she said. "It's sad, but kind of…welcome at the same time. Sad to think you'll carry it forever, but welcome because it means you'll never forget someone who should never be forgotten."

"Exactly."

"That's…very wise. Hard, but wise."

That earned her another glance. "Wisdom doesn't generally come easy."

"No. No, it doesn't."

She didn't tell him he'd surprised her with it. It was hardly flattering to know someone is surprised that one had such depths. But she had been, and she supposed that said more about her than him. She thought back to the days when she'd been in the throes of her crush on him, the days when she had suffered through feeling like that fifth wheel—not through anything he or Hope had said or done, but through her own insecurities—just to be around him. She remembered how she had surreptitiously watched him as much as possible, learning by heart the way his mouth quirked when he was mildly amused, the way his eyes crinkled when he smiled, the way he tilted his head slightly when he was curious or intrigued.

That last thought made her breath catch.

She couldn't help looking at him full on then, thankful the steep, curving road kept him focused on driving.

He had, she had just suddenly realized, been looking at her that way all day long.

Chapter 13

They'd gone into the market without a real plan, but after discovering that the little market had an actual butcher—a man they chuckled to find was the brother of Anson Woodruff and as opposite the voluble postmaster as it was possible to get, communicating mostly with grunts and hand gestures—they'd come out with a paper-wrapped stack of thick, wonderful-looking steaks.

Local grown, they'd managed to pry out of the taciturn Woodruff brother. Guaranteed.

"I wonder if he's like that because he was never able to get a word in edgewise around his brother?" Cara had said as they returned to the car.

Gabe had laughed out loud at the image that was summoned up in his mind. And realized, not for the first time, that despite the relative grimness of their task here, he'd laughed more today than he had in some time.

And he had the sudden thought that this, all of it, the drive here, the search, everything, would have been much, much grimmer had he not had Cara to share it with. He would have done it, certainly, there had been no choice about that, but the entire expedition would have been one of silent, enduring determination without her.

Distraction, he told himself as he put the dish now holding the steaks in the big fridge. That was the key, distraction.

They'd purchased a marinade Cara had recommended, and after testing the artfully combined flavors with a finger dipped in the blend, he'd seen why. The meat had a couple of hours to nicely soak up those flavors.

He'd liked the way she'd teased him about the manly art of grilling, seemingly quite happy to turn that part of the prep over to him when the time came. While she'd prepared greens for a salad he'd chopped an onion, and when she'd remarked on his technique—he'd gone to a cooking class with Hope once, in an effort to spend more time with her when he was ashore—he didn't even feel the pang he usually did when he thought of those times.

Yes, she was the perfect distraction, he thought again. Not someone brand-new that you felt awkward around, which would have only added to the stress, but at the same time, so much time had passed since they'd seen each other that there was plenty to talk about. That's all it was.

Be glad of the diversion and quit trying to analyze it, he told himself.

They'd brought in the personal necessities they'd bought at the near-miraculous general store, and Miriam, after declaring the steaks to be perfect, had shown them upstairs to two adjacent rooms.

The minute the doors swung open Gabe saw why they'd been named the green and blue rooms; they were identical in furnishings except for those colors. Miriam showed them the bathroom in between the two rooms, with access from both sides, and in the surprisingly spacious room the two colors collided in a cool blend of jewel tones.

"It's our family suite, so to speak," Miriam said with her charming laugh. "The most practical to keep available all the time."

"Efficient," Gabe noted.

"As is Crystal," Miriam said as if in further defense of her choice to keep the young woman around, indicating the tidiness and readiness of the rooms, "when she wants to be."

"It's good of you, to help her like this," Cara said.

"She earns her keep, contrary to appearances. And considering the life she's had, a runaway from an abusive home at fourteen, finding even worse on the streets for two years, being kidnapped, assaulted and dumped up here in the dead of winter, it's amazing she functions at all."

Gabe felt a spark of remorse at his reaction to Crystal. But at the same time, his suspicions sharpened; with that kind of history....

"I'll leave you to get settled in," Miriam said. "I hope you don't mind sharing the bathroom."

"Of course not," Cara said.

Gabe thanked Miriam, all the while keeping Cara in his peripheral vision. If she was actually bothered at the idea of sharing the bathroom they were standing in, it didn't show. She simply set down the toothbrush and small tube of toothpaste she'd purchased, then turned to look at him.

"Color preference?" she asked with a smile. "Or shall I just assume you want blue, for the sea?"

What I want would shock you, Cara Thorpe.

The words echoed in his head, and for a moment he held his breath, afraid he'd unknowingly spoken them aloud, so suddenly had they come upon him. As had the sudden vision of the different conversation they might be having if there weren't two rooms at the ready. The different conversation they might be having if the rest of the vivid images that had disquietingly popped into his head were more that just imagination.

Talk about shock. What the hell was he thinking? This was Cara.

And Cara was standing there looking at him, puzzlement beginning to show in her face as he didn't answer what must seem to her a simple question.

He quashed the unexpected, unwanted, and unwelcome—it

was all that, wasn't it?—response and reached for the cover of long-ago training in keeping his thoughts hidden. He leaned against the doorjamb and looked at her, noting he was managing to smile pleasantly.

"There are places," he said, "where the sea is as green as that wall is."

The smile she gave back, one of warmth mixed with appreciation and what seemed to be a touch of longing, blasted his attempt at cool nonchalance to bits. "And you've seen them all, haven't you?"

"Not all," he said, having to work to hide the sudden quickness of his breath as his usually steady, unflappable pulse took a leap. "Many."

"I'd like to hear about them, someday."

"I'd like to tell you about them. Someday."

And to his surprise, he meant it. He meant it, because he knew that in Cara he would have a listener who truly wanted to hear the tales, not one who would hear them grudgingly, resenting even as he spoke that those places he talked of had kept them apart.

Initially, he thought, it had been flattering that Hope had missed him so much. But what had been attractive in the beginning had eventually begun to wear him down; the constant feeling of guilt at abandoning her had gnawed at him relentlessly.

Hope just didn't have the resources to deal with being alone.

Cara's observation, and that she'd made it at all, had surprised him. As so many things had surprised him since Cara had reappeared in his life.

This afternoon.

That realization stunned him. Had it really only been a few hours? It seemed much longer. As if they'd picked up where they'd left off.

Well, not exactly, Gabe muttered inwardly. *You never had thoughts about her like you just had before.*

"The blue will be fine," he said abruptly, before any of those thoughts and vivid images could creep in and take hold again.

He turned as if to go toward the room he'd chosen, but stopped when Cara put a hand softly on his arm. He looked back at her.

"Thank you, Gabe."

His head drew back a little in surprise. "For what?"

"For being willing to do this. To go through this. For not just wanting to…ignore that card, when that would have been the easier thing to do."

He looked down into those vivid blue eyes. Saw the warmth and emotion there. His gut knotted up all over again, but this time for entirely different reasons.

"Easier, perhaps," he said, aware his voice sounded a bit rough, but unable to help it, "but at the same time, impossible."

"Yes. Impossible."

For a moment she just looked at him, and then an almost inaudible sigh escaped her. It was a tiny sound filled with so much remembered pain. With a sudden awareness that they were two people who had suffered a huge, mutual loss, he found himself doing what he hadn't done all those years ago, hadn't been able to do because he was so curled in on himself, smothered in pain and confusion and guilt.

He put his arms around Cara and pulled her into a gentle hug.

"If the answer's here, we'll find it, Cara," he said.

She had gone very still at his embrace, but when he spoke she relaxed, leaned against him, into him, taking the comfort he'd belatedly offered. The shared contact, the warmth, eased the old pain even more, and Gabe wondered that he hadn't realized it would do that.

"I should be thanking you," he said, lifting her chin up with a gentle finger. "For still caring so much after all this time."

"It could have been twice as long," she said. "It wouldn't make any difference."

He knew, saw in her eyes, that it was true. Cara Thorpe was loyal to the bone, and mere time could never change that.

He didn't even realize what he was doing until his lips brushed hers. It hadn't been a conscious decision, couldn't have been, for it was one he never would have made. But she was there, so close, looking up at him with that unwavering steadiness he realized he should have appreciated more, would have appreciated more had he known how important it was, back then.

And the next thing he knew, he'd done it. He'd kissed her.

And he couldn't regret it. Even when she backed away, startled, mumbled something about freshening up for dinner, and darted into the green room, closing the door behind her.

He stood there for a long moment. It hadn't really been a kiss, he told himself. Not really. Not a serious one. It had been more in the nature of a thank you, just a bit stronger than words. That's all.

She wasn't perfect. And what happened to her doesn't make her perfect.

He wasn't sure why Cara's words about Hope hit him just then, but they rang in his mind as if she'd still been standing here and had spoken them again.

"So we agree she wasn't perfect," he muttered as he turned and retreated to the blue room Cara had chosen for him. "That doesn't mean we give up trying to find out what happened."

He gave a sharp nod to the empty room, as if for emphasis. And ruefully recognized the voice in the back of his head saying, *That doesn't mean carte blanche for you to get crazy over Cara Thorpe, either, buddy.*

No, he thought, it doesn't.

But the acknowledgment didn't tell him how to deal with the unwelcome fact that Cara Thorpe had somehow stirred the first real interest he'd felt in a woman in longer than he cared to admit.

Thanks.

That's all it was, all it had been, no question. Just thanks, right? Hadn't he said as much? Hadn't that just been a hug shared between two friends who'd lost someone very special in their lives? And that kiss, it hadn't really been a kiss, not a romantic one, but just…something that meant more than words?

Hadn't it all, as always, been about Hope?

If there's no question, why are you asking so many? Cara wondered in rueful silence.

"Because he just blew you out of the proverbial water," she answered aloud, needing to hear the words, needing the sound to emphasize the absurdity of her own reaction to the barest brush of his lips over hers.

It was in thanks, nothing more, get that through your head, she ordered.

She busied herself with setting out the other things she'd bought, a large T-shirt to sleep in and a tiny bottle of soap to wash her underwear for the morning, checking her makeup, what little she wore, and, to her embarrassment, pulling, out of her hair a pine needle she'd obviously picked up somewhere.

She pulled her purse across the top of the dresser, and dug into it to bring out the folding hairbrush she carried. She used it thoroughly, in case there were more needles she couldn't see. The tree in front of the library building, she guessed, vaguely remembering a branch brushing her head.

She was this gorgeous, totally hot woman….

Greg's words came back to her now, doing more to clear her head of any silly ideas that that brief, startling kiss had brought on than any self-lecture had. For on some level she suspected the truth was that that hug, that kiss, had been more than just thanks.

It had been a way for Gabe to feel close to Hope again.

She stopped brushing. And for a moment she just looked at her reflection in the mirror. Yes, she looked better these days. More than acceptable.

But she was no Hope Taggert. She never would be.

And that, she told herself, was something she would do well to remember.

Chapter 14

For all his traveling the world, Gabe wasn't used to waking up in strange places.

In the service, his tidy, utilitarian quarters aboard ship had been his home away from home. Now he woke up inevitably in one of only two places, either his somewhat Spartan, if spacious apartment near the marina, or more often since she'd been launched, the new Redstone flagship.

He'd laughed at himself when he'd had to admit, after some good-natured teasing from the crew, that he was spending more time there than at home. He'd told himself the understated but definite luxury of the boat had lured him into the soft life, then had smiled because he didn't regret it.

But he knew it was simply being back on the water that had lured him. It was, he knew, in his blood, and likely would always be. And he would be forever thankful to Josh for giving him a chance to put the sea beneath him again, for as long as he wanted; he still oversaw the marine division of Redstone, but Josh was more than happy to let him do it from the bridge of the sleek, subtly elegant boat.

But when he woke up this morning, it wasn't simply the unfamiliar surroundings that disconcerted him. It wasn't even that the startling sound of a neighboring rooster had acted as an alarm clock.

It was the dream that rooster's raucous call had jolted him out of.

"Hope," he whispered.

Unlike so many mornings after her disappearance, he didn't say it with sadness, longing, or grief. Because this time, his dream had been different. This time, he'd dreamed of rising this morning, going downstairs to Miriam's cheerful kitchen, and finding his wife sitting there, alive, well, and none too happy to see him.

"Can't you take a hint, Gabe?" she'd asked, not bothering with a greeting first. "If I'd wanted you to find me, I would have left a trail."

He sat up, running a hand through his hair, then rubbing at his eyes. He hadn't slept well anyway, and this was just the capper. It was early, not even six, but he knew there was little chance he would go back to sleep, not now.

It wasn't the first time he'd dreamed of finding Hope. It wasn't even the first time he'd dreamed of finding her and discovering she'd walked away intentionally, without a qualm, wanting simply to be rid of him.

But it was the first time he'd dreamed it with the annoyingly tempting Cara Thorpe in the next room.

Tempting? Cara Thorpe?

The words seemed to glow in his mind as he swung out of the bed he'd had to sleep diagonally on; a double bed just wasn't enough for his height.

He rubbed his stubbled jaw as he headed for the bathroom. And stopped dead as he realized he'd been about to walk, buck naked, into a bathroom he was supposed to be sharing with that same, tempting, Cara Thorpe.

He fought down the images that thought brought on. Retreated and grabbed his jeans, yanking them on with little heed for other things that had risen at that thought. If it took a little pain to get himself back in line, so be it.

The bathroom was empty. The door to Cara's room was closed, and he walked over to click the lock so she wouldn't walk in on him the way he would have.

But she probably doesn't sleep naked, he thought.

And groaned as he had to start the quashing procedure all over again. And ordered himself not to speculate exactly what Cara slept in. Or not.

When he finally got around to standing in front of the mirror with the disposable razor and the small can of shaving cream he'd purchased, he thought he was back under control. They would talk to Miriam again today, he thought as he started to shave, and he would probe a little more into the irascible and more than a little suspicious Crystal. Despite Miriam's assurances, her attitude, apparent history, and the fact that she and Hope had been here at the same time was enough to put her on his list of inquiries.

It occurred to him suddenly that this was an area where St. John might be of help.

He finished quickly, toweled off the remaining specks of the shaving cream, checked for spots he'd missed and found none. Then he went back into the cool, blue room and picked up his cell phone. It was early, but everyone at Redstone knew that whatever hour you called, chances were St. John would be there. It was part of the legend that had built up around Josh's mysterious right-hand man.

And in fact, the man answered in the middle of the second ring. With Gabe's name, gleaned obviously from the caller ID.

"Taggert."

"Yes," Gabe confirmed, probably unnecessarily; the guy no doubt recognized his voice already. He paused for a split second, then remembered whom he was talking to and got right to business. "I need someone checked out."

"Go."

He gave what little information he had. "I don't know if that's her real name, or exactly how old she is, but she may have a criminal record. Car burglaries or the like."

"Description?"

St. John certainly hadn't become loquacious overnight, Gabe noted with a quirk of his mouth. He recited Crystal's hair color, height, and approximate age and weight, but ran into a problem when St. John wanted eye color and any identifying scars or marks. He'd been too focused on the young woman's attitude and obvious anger to notice.

Gabe heard a sound in the bathroom; Cara was apparently up. He hoped he hadn't disturbed her at this early hour. But then it struck him she might have noticed more than he had about Crystal; women tended to, didn't they?

He walked over and tapped on the bathroom door. There was a moment of silence before she called out an answer to the knock. She didn't open the door, and the question of exactly what stage of indecency she might be in battered at him anew.

"I'm talking to St. John," he said through the door. "He's going to check out Crystal, but he needs more description than I can give him. I thought maybe you noticed something I didn't. Like her eye color, at least."

"Oh." He heard some rustling, and then the door opened. "Brown," she said. "Very dark brown."

He realized now he'd seen her nightwear. He'd thought she purchased the souvenir T-shirt to wear today, but apparently she'd slept in it. The image emblazoned across the chest was actually of the lake a few miles away, but declared the village of Pine Lake the Gateway to Fun. The fact that the image also rested directly atop Cara's nicely rounded breasts didn't escape him.

He hadn't intended to but he handed her his cell phone. He didn't trust himself to say another word at the moment, not when his mind had just connected Cara's breasts with the words *"Gateway to Fun."*

She looked startled, but accepted the phone.

"Mr. St. John?"

It only took a moment for her to fall into the rhythm he guessed most people did when talking to the man. In self-defense, he supposed.

"Yes, dark brown." There was a pause just long enough for St. John to say his usual single word. "There was one thing. She had some marks on her left arm. A row of dots. Could have been scars. Like she'd had stitches at some point, or maybe screws holding a break." Another pause. "Yes, we'll try to find out. No, nothing else. Thank—"

Cara stopped mid-phrase.

"You," she finished to the air as she flipped the phone shut and handed it back to him. She lifted a brow at Gabe, the corresponding corner of her mouth quirked upward in an expression of bemusement.

"An experience, isn't it?" Gabe said, well back in hand now.

"One of a kind," Cara agreed.

"If he lives up to even half the reputation he has at Redstone, we'll have her entire history by this afternoon."

She smiled. Then took a step back. "I need to get ready."

It took him a moment to realize she meant he should back up and let her shut the bathroom door again. And he realized with a little jolt he had felt comfortable standing here like this, talking to her in what, to anyone, would seem like very intimate circumstances.

He backed up hastily. The glimpse he caught as she turned and closed the door reminding him of something he'd always known but had forgotten: Cara had legs that went on forever. She was at least six inches taller than the petite Hope had been, but it hadn't been until one day at the beach that he'd realized the difference was practically all in those long legs.

But they'd been skinny then, he thought. Now they were just…luscious.

He groaned inwardly at his own unruly thoughts and turned away.

He sat down on the edge of the bed to pull on his shoes and socks, concentrating as if he were a five-year-old who'd just learned how to do it. As a device to keep his thoughts in control, it didn't work very well. Hope had always said his ability to compartmentalize made her crazy, that she hated that he could just stop thinking about one important thing to focus entirely on another. It was, she admitted, more efficient, but she herself simply couldn't stop worrying about everything at once.

You'd laugh at me now, he said to the image in his mind. And then went still.

He doubted very much Hope would laugh if she knew the reason he was having so much trouble just now. And he wondered, if that dream were to come true and he went downstairs to find her alive and well in Miriam's kitchen, how would he feel?

He'd always assumed his life would right itself, instantly and automatically, the way a Coast Guard motor lifeboat did when capsized by heavy surf.

Now he wasn't so sure. *Especially* now.

Because if they found Hope, then what he'd been thinking and feeling about Cara Thorpe were completely out of line. And that the idea of Cara simply dropping out of his life again bothered him a great deal more than it should only emphasized that he was in water that was deeper than he'd realized.

Much deeper.

"Good morning to you both. Did you sleep well?"

The cheerful words of Miriam's greeting matched the sunlit kitchen today. But there was a sadness in her expression that told Cara she hadn't at all forgotten why the husband and best friend of the girl she'd taken under her wing were here.

"Fine," Cara said, noticing that Gabe didn't speak but let her answer stand for them both.

Efficiency again, she told herself, trying to quash the thought that popped into her head, of what it would be like to have first-hand knowledge of exactly how he'd slept.

It was just that moment this morning, when she'd had to open the bathroom door. She'd thought about running into the bedroom and quickly dressing, but from what he'd told her, the mysterious St. John wasn't someone you wanted to keep waiting. So she hadn't, and while Gabe had been scrupulously polite, she'd been very aware she was standing there in nothing but panties and the T-shirt she'd slept in.

And even more aware of the broad expanse of his bare chest, and the pattern of hair she'd never forgotten, tapering downward over his belly in a path she hadn't even known enough to want to follow when she'd first seen it, all those years ago.

She knew enough, now. And the idea took her breath away.

She was sure she'd been imagining, because of her self-consciousness, that his gaze had lingered on her breasts. Then again, he was a man—most definitely—and perhaps unable not to notice. It wasn't specific, it wasn't her….

Satisfied that she'd resolved that embarrassment, she gestured at the stack of papers sitting beside Miriam on the kitchen counter. "What's all this?"

"You said at dinner last night you hadn't seen any of Hope's work."

"No," Gabe said, and Cara heard the edge that came into his voice whenever this heretofore secret side of his wife's life came up, although it seemed a bit less strident this morning, as if he were gradually adjusting to the idea. As she hoped she herself was. They had talked at length last night about Hope's hidden— from them, at least—interest, and had found themselves fascinated by Miriam's stories of her career. If it were true Hope had harbored such a dream, it was easy to see why she would have been drawn to this woman.

Miriam gave Gabe a curious look. "She must have kept copies of her work at home, for herself?"

Gabe shook his head. "She had her own laptop. It disappeared when she did. And I…when I was home, computers weren't what I was home for."

"I see," Miriam said. "In that case."

She nudged the stack of printed pages toward them. The obvious indication that these were Hope's writings gave Cara a chill. She gave Gabe a sideways glance. He was staring at the half-inch stack of pages with an odd expression, part anticipation, part apprehension and something else she couldn't name. Considering her own tangled emotions as she looked at those pages, she wasn't surprised he was feeling something similar.

But before either of them could bring themselves to look, there was a bang as the back door slammed open. Crystal again.

"Still here."

It wasn't really a question, and since the answer was so readily apparent, no one, even Miriam, seemed to feel compelled to answer it. Nor did Crystal seem to expect an answer; she just strode through the kitchen toward them.

Cara felt Gabe tense beside her, and wondered what he was thinking. Did he feel the rough-edged, angry young woman was really a threat?

Crystal skirted them almost warily, as if she'd sensed Gabe's sudden alert readiness. Perhaps she had; if she'd lived on the streets as Miriam had said, then she likely had some finely honed survival instincts. And anyone would be well advised to be wary of Gabriel Taggert on alert, Cara thought.

The young woman, wearing worn jeans and a denim jacket over a cropped T-shirt that revealed a rather sloppy circular tattoo of barbed wire around her navel, stopped beside Miriam. She crossed her arms in front of her, in a stance that was almost aggressive. In an odd way, it seemed as if she were putting herself between the woman who had taken her in and these two intruders, as if she felt they were a threat.

Miriam smiled at the angry young woman as if she were a well-behaved, charming daughter.

"Yes, dear?"

"Finished the shed."

"Why, thank you, Crystal."

"Found that broken easel. I'll work on it."

"That would be very helpful." Miriam paused, then gestured at Gabe and Cara. "Isn't there something you'd like to say?"

For an instant surprise registered on Crystal's sharp features. "What?"

"It was thoughtful of them to include you in their dinner plans last night, don't you think?"

They had discussed that when they'd bought the steaks. Cara had finally suggested they buy enough to include Crystal, and if there were leftovers, steak and eggs in the morning was always an option. With a comment about feeding the bears in the woods, Gabe had agreed. Crystal had, in fact, not joined them, but she had taken the extra steak and vanished to wherever it was she holed up.

"Oh."

When nothing else came, Miriam prompted gently. "One usually thanks people for such thoughtfulness."

Crystal flicked a glance at Miriam. Cara watched her expression, looked for anything that indicated emotion behind the stiff facade. She saw nothing—no gentleness, no affection—for this generous woman who had taken her in.

But there was no anger, either, not like the kind she'd seen directed at everyone else. Cara supposed that was something.

But when Crystal looked back at them, the usual resentment was in place as she glowered. "Thanks for the food."

Without another word she turned sharply on the heel of her run-down motorcycle boot and stalked back out the way she'd come in. Miriam didn't comment further on her appearance or manner, so Cara assumed what they'd seen was typical.

Perhaps Gabe was right to be on guard, she thought. That woman could definitely be trouble.

And then, far too belatedly, something struck her. Was Gabe thinking much more specifically than just a general wariness of this woman?

Was he thinking she had something to do with Hope's disappearance?

The possibility that had always and ever hovered, like a threatening thunderstorm, that Hope was not only dead, but had been murdered, slammed into Cara's consciousness with a fierceness that nearly made her gasp. Involuntarily she turned to look at the door Crystal had exited through.

Could she?

No doubt.

Would she?

Maybe.

Had she?

Cara shivered.

And suddenly the pleasant kitchen didn't seem quite so sunny.

Chapter 15

Cara was still shivering in response to her own thoughts about Crystal when, unexpectedly, she felt Gabe's hand at her back, warm, strong, comforting. As if he'd felt her reaction and wanted to ease it. She barely managed not to turn and look at him.

"You take a look at these, and I'll fix us some breakfast. The least I can do after that lovely dinner last night," Miriam said.

Cara took a seat on the same stool she'd used before. Gabe sat beside her, still looking warily at the papers Miriam had printed out, as if they were a coiled snake. Cara understood the feeling, felt more than a little of it herself, but curiosity finally overcame it and she began to read.

The pages contained, as Miriam had told them last night, short character sketches and *slice-of-life* pieces. The images they brought up were vivid, and Hope's charm and liveliness fairly leaped off the page. Cara smiled as from one she recognized Mr. Matton, their mutual sixth grade teacher; the portrait was sharp and funny, and she thought that anyone reading it would understand what it was like to have been in his over-bearing grip.

She set the pages she finished in front of Gabe. It took him, she noticed, until the third one to actually pick up the first and start reading. But he did, and she wondered if that meant he'd won the battle with himself, or lost it.

Miriam set plates of eggs and ham before them, then discreetly left them to their task. They ate, but their attention was focused on the papers. It was as if Hope were there with them, so clearly did her personality show in the writing.

"Her parents," Cara murmured as she began the next set of pages. And when she'd finished, she looked up at Hope's husband. "Oh, Gabe, they must see this. It's so full of her love for them."

He took the pages she held out, and this time began reading immediately. She watched him, the memory fresh in her mind of what had been written on the page about the solid, steady pair who had raised and loved their beautiful little girl. She knew where he was in the piece by the way he smiled here and there, knew he'd gotten to the part about their unconditional love by the way he swallowed as if his throat were tight.

"You're right," he said softly when he finished. "They have to see this."

Pleased, she returned to the next in the stack. And then her breath caught as she realized what it was, a paean to Hope's best friend.

Cara felt her insides knot as she read Hope's words. *Cara's my rock. She's always there for me. She doesn't just listen to me, she* hears *me. She always has.*

She read on until the words blurred, as if the printed ink had smeared.

"Cara?"

Gabe's voice was gentle, and she realized that tears were streaming down her face.

He slipped from his seat on the stool beside her and put his arms around her. She leaned into him, heedless of anything except that, at this moment, she needed this comfort so desperately it didn't matter that he was the husband of the very woman who'd brought her to this state.

"I miss her," she choked out. "So much."

"I know," Gabe said softly.

She leaned against him, trying to control her weeping. Finally, she managed to choke back the next sob, then the next.

"I'm sorry. I didn't mean to—"

"Shh. I know."

She lapsed into silence then, her head still pressed against his strong, broad chest. Gradually she became aware of the comforting warmth of him, and that she could hear the solid, steady thud of his heart.

The heart Hope had joked never beat faster than sixty-two beats per minute, no matter the provocation.

"Never?" Cara had asked archly.

Hope had grinned at her, not missing the implication. "Well, there's always one exception to prove the rule."

In that moment Cara had regretted her own teasing. The innuendo was clear, and it had given rise to images in her fevered, infatuated imagination that she would rather not have had. And she'd seen just enough of Gabe, on the occasional trips to the beach where at Hope's insistence she had joined them, to fill in the blanks. Vividly.

Those images flooded her mind now, as clear and vivid as they had been back then. More so, in fact, since at the moment the star of those images had his arms around her. And she'd recently seen that broad, bare chest up close and personal.

The fact that he was trying to comfort her despite emotions of his own that had to be roiling with the discovery of these papers, the fact that he was the husband of the woman who had been her best friend and who had written this glowing testament to that friendship, the fact that they were still no closer to knowing what had happened, made her own reluctance to pull away from him seem embarrassingly inappropriate.

He's Hope's, she said silently, then repeated it with more emphasis. It had been the only thing that had worked, back in the days when she'd found herself looking at him with such longing she was terrified it must show. It would work now, she told herself.

Except…she wasn't who she'd been, back in those days.

And Hope isn't here.

The words ringing in her ears as if she'd spoken them, felt like a betrayal, especially coming on the heels of reading the piece that Hope had written about her, about her best friend, the one person she trusted more than anyone in the world and always had.

Fine way to deserve that trust, Cara thought as she pulled out of Gabe's embrace abruptly. He seemed surprised at her sudden movement, but he didn't try to stop her.

She fought to steady herself. "I'm all right. Thank you."

It came out stiffly, formally, as if he'd been a stranger who'd held open a door for her. She tried for a more normal tone. Gestured toward the pages she'd dropped when she'd no longer been able to read through her tears.

"It was just that she wrote this about me and it…."

"Caught you off guard?"

Glad he seemed to have accepted her explanation, she nodded. "I'll…finish that one later." *When I'm alone and can cry my eyes out and not turn to my best friend's husband for comfort.*

"May I read it now?"

Oddly, he sounded as stiff and formal as she had moments ago. She hesitated; Hope's praise—and her prediction of what Cara could become, if only she had more confidence—had been unstinting. Almost embarrassing, because no matter how far she'd come, she couldn't believe she'd come far enough to fulfill Hope's vision. But Gabe already had the pages in his hand, and she didn't feel she had the right to ask him not to read it, even though he'd asked. If anyone had the right to any and everything Hope, it was Gabe.

She gave up on finishing breakfast and pushed the plate out of the way still half-full of food. She had the feeling Miriam would understand.

She looked at the next page, the start of a story of Hope's first hair-raising drive up the mountain, and how she'd gradually become used to the steep, curving roads and come to love the adventure of it enough to seek out other roads to follow, to explore. Cara remembered their own drive up, and Hope's descriptions were so vivid it was like doing it all over again.

Gabe would like that one, she thought as she passed it over to him to read. He was still reading Hope's essay about her. And he was smiling, even nodding slightly. In agreement? she wondered. That thought took her breath away all over again, and she told herself he was simply responding to the fact that the words had been written by Hope.

She stared down at the next page she had, unseeingly, as Gabe continued to read. But after a moment something drew her attention and she focused on the printed words before her.

The next sketch was about Gabe. It was his name that had caught her eye.

She looked away quickly, not sure she wanted to read this. Then back at the page, which began with the words, "Only love can make you so happy and so angry at the same time."

She glanced at the rest of the first page, saw the description of Gabe, the "tall, dark and handsome" cliché plus a string of other descriptors like smart, sexy, brave, and generous. None of which Cara could argue with.

But Hope had also expressed anger here, and hurt, bemoaning his long absences and describing him as stubborn, single-minded, and sometimes thoughtless. Cara couldn't argue with those, either, although she would have amended the last to "belatedly thoughtful" rather than thoughtless; Gabe might be late in understanding sometimes, but once he did, he moved fast to catch up. How often had she envied Hope the way Gabe admitted minor offenses by going overboard to make up for them? How often had she wanted to tell Hope she was a fool, to zero in on such small failings when there was so much more that was positive?

And how was Gabe going to feel to read this?

She gave him a sideways glance. But he wasn't looking at her, he'd finally moved on to the next piece, so she slid the essay about him down to the bottom of the stack. She wouldn't hide it from him, but she could delay it.

When he put down the pages he held, he looked both thoughtful and…weary, Cara realized suddenly. And she realized she, too, was tired, not physically, but in that way that made even the simplest thought difficult.

"I need to clear my head," Gabe said, just as she'd been about to say something very similar.

"Yes," she agreed. "There's been a lot to take in since yesterday."

"I want to go down the mountain a bit. To that gas station we passed."

"You think she might have gone there?"

"It's the only one around, as far as I could tell. Chances are she did at some point."

They explained to Miriam before they left, who, as Cara had expected, understood. "It must be painful to read those. It will be for me, too, now." She shook her head sadly. "The writers I know tend to be introverted, solitary types. Hope was such a breath of fresh air."

Gabe asked about the gas station and Miriam nodded, confirming his guess that it was the only one in or near town.

"I remember at least once Hope saying she needed to fill up before she started home. And Stan's owned that place since it opened." She smiled. "He's also a bit of a harmless flirt, and I can't imagine he wouldn't have flirted with a woman who looked like Hope."

Gabe said nothing to that, merely nodded. Perhaps he'd been used to such things, Cara thought. If you married a woman like Hope, she supposed you would have to be.

By tacit agreement they left their things at the inn, meaning to come back. "I want to finish reading," Cara said as they got into the car, "but it's…too much right now."

"I know," Gabe said. "It's like she was there, in the room, looking over my shoulder."

"Exactly," Cara said, glad she didn't have to explain why she felt she had to take a break.

Gabe fastened his seat belt, and Cara pulled hers out to do the same. As she twisted to do so she saw, just past the corner of the inn, Crystal standing with a man she'd never seen before. As usual, she looked belligerent, while the man looked annoyed.

"It must be awful to wake up like that every day," she said when she saw that Gabe had noticed them as well.

"I'd be careful, if I were him," Gabe said, sounding as if he were only half joking. "She's armed."

Cara blinked, then realized he meant the pair of garden clippers the woman held. As she pointed them at the man in an angry gesture, Cara's own earlier thoughts about Crystal's potential for violence came rushing back to her. But in that instant the woman turned on her heel and stalked away. The man she'd been talking to glanced around, shaking his head as they had more than once after running afoul of Crystal's unpleasant demeanor.

As they left the little town, she tried to remember exactly how far down the gas station was. She remembered noticing it—and the higher prices that no doubt reflected the difficulty of getting the commodity up here—but couldn't recall how much farther it had been before they'd hit the main street of Pine Lake.

"I wonder if he thought Pine Lake would eventually spread this far," Gabe said, as if he'd been thinking similar thoughts.

"Maybe," she said. "Or maybe he picked the spot to serve more than just Pine Lake."

"Could be," Gabe agreed. "There's that place we passed the turnoff to, on the way up here. The one Hope mentioned when she wrote about driving up here."

He spoke evenly, as if he were referring to nothing more than some travel guide. And in the face of the neutral tone, Cara couldn't think of a thing to say.

"I want to check that out," Gabe went on. "She said it was one of the first places she went exploring."

"I wondered about that," Cara said. "If we should go there and do the same thing we did in Pine Lake."

"I think so. It's someplace she actually went, so she might have talked to people there."

"Hope always talked to people," Cara agreed.

"I think we should—"

He stopped suddenly, frowning. His hands shifted on the steering wheel. Tightened around it.

And then he swore, low and harsh under his breath.

"What?" Cara asked, turning in her seat to look at him.

"The power steering just went out."

Cara's eyes widened. She remembered once trying to steer a car with a dead battery down a driveway, how next to impossible it had been to control without the assist of the power steering.

She looked around. Her heart began to hammer in her chest.

They were on a steep, curving mountain road. With drop-offs that took your breath away.

In a car that was going to fight making every turn.

At least he had brakes, Gabe thought as he muscled the vehicle he'd bought as a road car but now couldn't help thinking was a brick with wheels, into the next turn.

The smart thing would be to stop right here and now...except they were on a narrow, blind curve that could get them killed as quickly as going over the edge. And after that came another curve, back in the other direction, this one masked with trees that would make it nearly impossible for a car traveling at normal speed to see them in time to stop or dodge.

The wheel jerked under his hands as they went over an uneven stretch of road. He was aware of Cara's tension, but thankfully she said nothing as he worked to find the balance; the slower they went, the safer, but at the same time the slower they went, the harder the car became to steer.

He considered again simply stopping, but as if in answer a big sedan came ripping up behind them, at what appeared to be a frightening speed now that they'd slowed. It darted around them with horn blaring, cutting it so close Gabe heard Cara smother a gasp. He quickly activated the hazard lights.

Down on the flat, it wouldn't be a problem; the car was hard to steer but not at all impossible. Up here, on a narrow, steep road, control was critical.

He felt the tension building in his shoulders and hoped he was right in his guess that the gas station was close. They rounded two more turns, the usually responsive car protesting every inch of the way.

And then there it was, the brightly colored Plexiglas sign of the station. Gabe let out a compressed breath as he wrested the car off the road, lined it up with the single service bay beside the main building, and finally, gratefully, put full pressure on the brakes.

A man in a surprisingly clean uniform shirt bearing the name "Stan" and a handlebar moustache that Gabe figured he had to have been growing for years was headed toward them before they came to a complete stop.

"Problem?" the man said as Gabe hit the hood release before he opened the door and got out. "She looked like she was turning a little sluggish when you pulled in."

Flirt or not, the man got credit for noticing, Gabe thought. He obviously knew his stuff.

"Power steering went out," Gabe said, walking around to the front of the car and lifting the hood. For a moment what he was seeing didn't register. He blinked, shifted his angle, but that didn't change what he now had to accept. The reservoir that should have been full to the marking on the side was empty.

"That's not good," the moustached man said. "Nice car like this, too." There was a hint of censure in his voice, as if he suspected Gabe wasn't worthy of driving it.

"What is it?"

Cara had walked to the front of the car to join them. Stan looked up from the engine compartment, and at his first glimpse of Cara, a wide smile appeared below the carefully cultivated moustache.

"Well, now," he said.

Gabe hid his annoyance; he couldn't blame the guy, after all. "Power steering fluid's gone," he said in answer to her question. "And it was fine on Sunday. I check fluids every week," he added pointedly, with a sideways look at Stan. It didn't matter, the man was so intent on Cara that Gabe doubted he heard a word.

After a brief hello, and a smile that made Stan's widen, Cara leaned to look into the engine compartment. She quickly found the plastic reservoir, he noticed, and frowned as he had when she saw it was empty.

"Isn't that…unusual?" she asked.

"Very," piped up Stan.

Something caught Gabe's eye, made his gaze narrow. Something glistening, wet where there shouldn't be any wetness; the road had been dry all the way. He backed up and dropped to the ground, scooting underneath the car to search for further sign of the gleam he'd seen.

He didn't have to look far. Something had sprayed all over the underside of the engine compartment. He reached up, ran a finger over the nearest piece of sheet metal, collecting some of the liquid. He already knew, but seeing the reddish cast of the fluid confirmed it.

"Flashlight," he said, a little sharply as something else caught his attention. "In the glove box."

He heard somebody move, then Cara's slim arm stuck the small light within his reach.

"Thanks," he said as he twisted it on. He looked, touched, and clenched his jaw.

He worked his way out from under, handed the flashlight to Stan. Something in his expression must have gotten through to the man, because he quit flirting with Cara and without another word duplicated Gabe's actions and got under the car.

When he came out, he looked as grim as Gabe was feeling.

"No doubt?" Gabe asked, looking at Stan.

"No doubt," the man said flatly.

"What is it?" Cara asked, looking only at Gabe. He hesitated, but then gave her the truth.

"The line was cut."

Chapter 16

"St. John says her real name is Linda Sparks. She's twenty-four. The story's pretty much as Miriam told us."

"Grim," Cara said.

"Yes," Gabe agreed.

But the grimness of the young woman's story didn't change one simple fact. Less than fifteen minutes after they'd seen her with garden clippers in her hand, they came near to having what could have been fatal trouble on a steep mountain road because of a cut fluid line.

The sheriff's deputy who had come out to look agreed with them that the line appeared to have been cut. He also, as Gabe had expected, said just seeing Crystal—or Linda—with a pair of garden clippers wasn't enough evidence. Not, he admitted, that he'd be surprised; he'd had a run-in or two with the woman himself. He'd look into it, he promised, and file the report, but he couldn't promise them any action in a hurry. They were still on their own, and Gabe wasn't sure he wasn't happier with it that way.

He'd gotten the call about Crystal from St. John, who'd given the information in his usual manner while Stan had been working on the car. Replacing the entire line was far more complicated than a simple fix, Gabe thought, but he didn't want to take any chances with a temporary repair not holding, not on these roads. And Stan seemed efficient and knowledgeable enough, once he'd stopped flirting with Cara.

Gabe looked over at her, sitting on the bench outside the gas station office. The sun had come out, and she'd turned her face upward as if welcoming the warmth in the brisk mountain air. She'd closed her eyes, so he felt he could look his fill.

The sunlight washed over her, and coppery sparks glinted in her hair. Now, in profile, he could see the slight upward tilt of her nose, the long sweep of her lashes, the set of the chin he'd thought of back then as so determined for such a quiet girl.

So different from Hope, he thought, but in a subtle, restrained way and now just as attractive. Hope had been right about that.

Gabe heard the clank of metal on metal. Stan muttered something from under the car, but kept working.

Stan had remembered Hope, of course. *Gorgeous little blonde,* he'd said. *A real charmer.*

All of which was true. Unfortunately, that's about all Stan remembered. She'd been in a couple of times for gas, and Stan, gentleman that he was, had waived the self-serve policy to fill the tank himself.

No sense a pretty girl like that smelling of gasoline, he'd said.

The one useful thing he'd been able to tell them was that Hope had asked about Morton's Corner, the place he and Cara had just been talking about.

"Told her there was nothing there but a little general store and a tavern, but she wanted to go," Stan had said, shaking his head. "Said she was exploring."

Another mutter came from under the car now, but Gabe saw that he had the old line out and was starting to put in the replacement. Gabe was grateful that Stan's repair bay was well stocked, and even if it wasn't a dealer-supplied part, he'd had something that would fit.

And next time he parked the car, even at a seemingly safe place like Miriam's, he'd set the car alarm no matter how much the thing irritated him when it went off. Not that it would help if the tampering was confined to the exterior; because the alarm annoyed him, he'd had the dealer set the sensitivity very low.

"Do you think she did it?"

Cara's words startled him; he'd thought she was just soaking up the sun. He should have realized she'd never stopped thinking. This was Cara, after all.

"I don't know."

That her mind had gone the same direction his had didn't surprise him. They'd been in synch on so much of this. She opened her eyes and turned to look at him then.

"What now?" she asked.

He'd been thinking about that. "I think when Stan's finished, we continue over to Morton's Corner." He gave her a sideways look. "And we take our time about it."

It didn't take her long. "And then, when it's been long enough that…whoever did this thinks they succeeded, we go back to Miriam's?"

He nodded, pleased but not surprised at her quickness. "And watch for reaction from Ms. Lowden-Sparks."

Cara nodded. "All right." Then, after a moment, she said with a note of sadness, "If she did do it, it's going to be very painful for Miriam."

"I know." He hesitated, decided it was nothing Cara hadn't already thought of, and added, "And it will be even worse for her if it turns out she had something to do with Hope's disappearance, too."

"She looks familiar," the woman putting boxes of macaroni and cheese on a shelf said as she peered at the photograph Cara held. "But she's not from around here."

"No," Cara agreed. "She would have only been visiting. But she wrote about coming here."

"Don't get many tourists out this far," the woman said. "Almost all of my business is locals, that's the only reason I remember her at all. Sorry I can't be more specific. But eight years ago…."

She left the obvious unspoken. But she was clearly not without sympathy. And, Cara thought as the woman eyed Gabe, appreciation for a fine-looking man.

"You could go talk to Charlie Taylor," she said. "He was the deputy sheriff around here for twenty-five years. He lives just up the hill. Drove all the way down on the flat to the sub-station to work, but said he loved it here too much to move closer. But him being the kind who notices things…."

They found the retired sheriff on his back deck tying fishing flies. He looked younger than Cara had expected, perhaps mid-fifties. He had salt-and-pepper hair cut in a short, brush cut Cara guessed he'd probably worn for decades. But on his upper lip was a moustache that made her wonder if he was competing with Stan for who could grow the longest handlebar.

He wore aviator-style glasses, but behind them his dark eyes were quick and alert as he looked at the photograph. "No, afraid she doesn't look familiar. Not a woman I'd forget, either." His gaze shifted to Gabe and he added in a tone that was more speculative than envious, "But if you were married to her, I reckon you're used to hearing that."

"She usually made an impression," Gabe said, apparently taking no offense.

"You say she came up here a lot?"

"To Pine Lake," Cara answered. "We're not sure if she came here more than once. We only know because she mentioned coming here, when she was writing about exploring the area."

"Exploring?"

Gabe began to explain, and Cara looked around. The deck they stood on was large and took advantage of the contour of the mountain to gain a view over an expanse of trees and sky. It must be lovely to just sit out here and soak it in, she thought. There was a fireplace built into one end of the deck that would let you be outside in all but the worst weather, she thought, and that sounded lovely as well. She'd lived as near the water as she could afford most of her life, but she could feel the appeal of this quiet, peaceful place.

"—roads. Happens all the time. Sometimes we never find them."

Cara abruptly tuned back in, feeling she should have been paying more attention.

"Never?" Gabe was asking, and there was an edge in his tone that told her this could be important.

"Sometimes," Taylor repeated sadly. "We'd get calls, about a crash in the night. Sound carries funny up here, echoes off the mountains, and if it's foggy it's even worse. You'd get a half-dozen calls about the sound of a crash, and every one of them would give you a completely different location, each one positive that's where it was. We'd check them all, but sometimes we never found a thing."

Cara stared at him. "You mean there could be people who were never found?"

"Can't say it doesn't happen." he shrugged at what Cara thought was a horrific idea. "More often, there are accidents where people went on their way. We'd find skid marks on the road sometimes, but no sign anybody didn't just drive away under their own power. That's not to say there weren't times we found nothing."

He seemed to realize Cara was aghast, and smiled at her. "Sorry, miss," he said. "It sounds callous, I know, but when you've been at this as long as I was, thirty-five years if you count my time down on the flat, you get to where you can't work up a sweat over things like you used to. Usually means it's time to get out."

"Is that what you did?" she asked.

He nodded. "It's a job where you had to care. I was too close to not being able to."

"Then congratulations on knowing when you had to get out or lose yourself," Gabe said. "It's a tough call."

Cara went quiet, knowing Gabe had spoken out of a fellow feeling Taylor would surely understand. The older man looked at Gabe, and after a moment nodded.

"That it is."

Even Cara could sense the quiet understanding that passed between the two men. Two men who, while wearing different uniforms, had held similar goals; the protection of those they served. Instead of feeling excluded by the masculine camaraderie, she felt uplifted, as if the world could never be a truly out-of-control place with men like this in it to stand against those who favored chaos.

They were back in the car and headed down Charlie's steep hill before Gabe said quietly, "I'd give a lot to know what you've been thinking."

Caught, Cara flushed. "I…it wasn't about this. Looking for Hope, I mean."

"I'd still like to know."

"I…" Lord, she was going to sound so corny. But he'd said it so quietly, so gently, that she couldn't doubt he really meant it. "I was just thinking about you and Deputy Taylor…and others like you. Who take a stand, I mean. You're why the world doesn't just…spin out of control."

Gabe slowed the car at the stop sign marking the intersection with the road that led back to the highway. When they were at a halt, he looked over at her. There was something warm and welcoming in his eyes, and in his voice when he said, simply, "Thank you."

"We—I mean the people you do it for—we don't thank you enough."

"You pay the price," he said, and turned back to his driving.

And Cara knew they were suddenly back to Hope, who, whatever her lack of understanding or appreciation for the bigger picture, had indeed done just that. Isolation and unhappiness had been the two things Hope had been least equipped to handle.

That there had been resources available to her wouldn't have mattered, Cara thought in one of those moments of assessment that made her feel so guilty now that her friend was gone. But she knew it was true; Hope wanted what she wanted, her husband with her, and no amount of assistance in how to cope with his absence would have changed that. In fact, Cara realize now, she probably would have resented it.

"She never should have married you," Cara said, voicing what in her heart she'd known for a very long time. "It wasn't fair to you."

"I can't argue with the first part," Gabe said, that harsh edge creeping back into his voice. He made the turn onto the winding road that had brought them to Charlie's.

"Then don't argue with the second, either. It's true, Gabe. You were honest with her, you told her what it would be like. If she chose to ignore all that, that wasn't your fault."

He glanced at her then, and she saw something in his expression she'd never seen before, a sort of speculation that made her pulse pick up speed.

"What would you have done, Cara? In her place, if you felt the way she had?"

In her place? Where I wanted to be with all my silly, young heart? I wouldn't have felt that way, she thought. *I would have been so proud of you it wouldn't have mattered.*

"I would have been first in line at the fleet counselor's office," Cara said, knowing he was waiting for an answer. Her mouth quirked. "I probably would have had a little trouble with the rank thing spilling over onto the families, but…."

She shrugged. She was afraid to go on, afraid she'd slip and let out how much she had longed for exactly that, to be in Hope's place, how furious she had been with her best friend for how she was reacting, how she'd barely managed to keep from erupting at her more than once, probably doing irrevocable damage to the friendship.

So instead she'd held it in, tried to speak of it only when she thought she could maintain control, and tell Hope she should be thankful, not resentful, that Gabe was the kind of man he was.

"It's a unique world," Gabe admitted as he slowed for a particularly sharp curve in the road. "And sometimes the unwritten rules are more important than the things in the regs. Hope always struggled with that. She hated that she couldn't even go to the doctor without having to give them all my information. Said it made her feel like an appendage, not an individual."

"I know. I heard all about it. I tried to point out they had to keep track of things somehow, but she didn't want to hear that."

Gabe said nothing to that, but Cara thought he was focused on driving at this moment. They were at a place she'd noticed on the way up, where the road nearly doubled back on itself in a rather hair-raising switchback. She remembered being glad then that she hadn't been the one driving. She wasn't particularly afraid of heights, but it was a scary spot.

She thought of what Deputy Taylor had said, and as she looked over the side into thick trees that somewhat masked what she knew had to be a horrendous drop-off, she suppressed a shiver. It would be so easy to go over, and in a little car like Hope's, the trees would just close back up around you, hiding you as surely as if you'd vanished underwater.

And if their own power steering had gone out now....

"That'd be my pick," Gabe said grimly when they were through the turn.

It took her a moment to realize his thoughts had gone in the same direction hers had.

"'Times we found nothing,'" she quoted softly, her throat tight.

Cara said nothing more, because the look on Gabe's face told her he was wrestling with images similar to the ones racing unstoppably through her head, none of them pleasant, some of them horrific.

He didn't speak again until they were at the main road, where the road to Morton's Corner met the highway, at the intersection where Stan's gas station stood.

"I need to make a call," he said, and turned once more into the station and parked. "I couldn't get a signal up there."

Stan again approached immediately, and Gabe quickly assured him things were fine, and thanked him once more for a job well done. Another customer drew the man to the gas pumps—self-serve was apparently open to interpretation for Stan—and left them alone.

Cara wondered if there was someone he wanted to call, after what could have been a narrow escape. Since they had a cell signal here, she would have thought he would have called before, while the car was being worked on, but maybe he had wanted to calm down first.

As *she* should, she told herself, embarrassed at how the idea of him with someone else still had the power to unsettle her. Just because he hadn't remarried after Hope didn't mean he wasn't involved. It might have been awkward, when Hope had never been declared legally dead, and as far as she knew he'd never filed for a divorce on whatever grounds he had, under the circumstances, but what woman wouldn't put up with a few complications for a man like Gabe?

"Do you want privacy?" Cara asked, one hand on the door handle, when he didn't use the hands-free phone system on the Lexus.

Gabe blinked. "What? No. I'm calling St. John." He saw her glance at the controls for the hands-free system. "I only use that when I'm actually driving," he explained. "Feels too weird talking into space if I don't have to."

"Oh. I thought maybe…."

Her voice trailed off. *Now that was awkward,* she thought, and felt her cheeks heat.

"No," he said, in an odd tone that made her wonder just what she'd sounded like. "There's…no one to call. Not like that. I—"

He broke off as the call went through. Cara was grateful for the distraction, wondered if she'd ever stop feeling like a fool in front of this man.

In the brief, succinct manner Cara imagined was typical for anyone talking to St. John, Gabe explained the situation. When he disconnected less than two minutes later, without a goodbye, Cara waited for and got the bemused expression again, the expression she imagined most people wore after a conversation— if you could call it that—with the man.

"He said they've got something that will help," Gabe said as he closed the phone. "He'll get back to me."

"Only he said it in five words or less?" Cara suggested.

Gabe looked at her. One corner of his mouth quirked upward in that lopsided smile she'd always loved.

"'There's something…be in touch,' I think is how it came out," he agreed.

"Amazing," she said as he put the phone away and put his hands back on the wheel.

"Now," he said with a grimness that wiped away the touch of humor, "let's go see if Crystal-Linda is surprised to see us alive."

Chapter 17

Cara didn't question him when he parked out of sight down the road from the inn, in the driveway of a small cabin that looked as if it hadn't been lived in for years. And he didn't bother to explain; it seemed clear she understood he wanted as much of the element of surprise as they could manage, and they had a much better chance of that if no one saw them drive up and stroll through the expansive garden.

She kept up with him as they made their way up the hill, and he noticed he didn't have to shorten his stride much for her to do it.

"There's a gate around on the side there. Looks like it goes through to the back, where the shed is," Cara said as they neared the wood fence that ran along the edge of the old inn property.

"Good idea," he said, and they changed direction.

The gate was a rather elaborate wrought-iron affair Gabe imagined required a bit of upkeep. Upkeep that hadn't been done, he thought, as he noted rusty patches on the bottom crossbar, and one spot where it had rusted completely through.

But his observations of the gate were cut short by the sound of voices. Raised voices. One of them male.

And the other was Crystal's, he was sure of it.

He saw Cara glance at him, but she didn't speak, just waited. He leaned forward to where he could see into the yard behind the old inn. The people talking weren't visible, but the voices seemed to be coming from the vicinity of the garden shed that sat across from the back door Crystal had come through when they were in the kitchen. He couldn't hear the words, just the angry tone.

He reached out to the gate's latch; it lifted easily. He nudged at the gate, testing for noise, but the tiny squeak didn't seem as if it would be audible beyond a few feet. Certainly not as far away as Crystal and her companion were, and not over their raised voices. He pushed it open the rest of the way.

Without comment Cara kept close, understanding the need for silence to get the result they wanted. Keeping to the edge of the path rather than the stepping stones, they made their way along the side of the inn toward the voices. With a quick glance and a nod at each other, they rounded the corner of the building together, then stopped.

It was definitely Crystal. She was up in the face of the man standing opposite her. The same man, Gabe noted, that she'd been arguing with before. And she was furious. So angry her face was distorted with it, red and blotchy. At this moment, there was no doubt in his mind that this woman could do something ugly.

And in that moment she did. She swung the handle of the rake she was holding at the man before her, with clear intent to do, at the least, bodily harm. Gabe heard Cara suck in an audible breath, weighed his options for a split second, decided there really were none, and moved.

In the same moment Cara moved with him, and he said under his breath, "Let me take her."

She didn't argue, apparently seeing the sense in him tackling the woman with the big stick and she the man who, while unknown, would presumably not fight with a woman, not to mention a total stranger. He spared a brief thought for the fact that she was—not surprisingly—cool in a pinch, and then he was focused on disarming the enraged Crystal.

If he'd wanted to know if she'd be surprised to see him, the look on her face gave him the answer. He realized, however, that it could be simply that, in her view, he'd appeared out of nowhere and wrenched her weapon out of her hands. She swore at him at the same moment he heard another oath from the man she'd been yelling at, who was no doubt wondering who they were.

"What the hell?"

He couldn't look at the man, not when Crystal was over her initial shock and glaring at him.

"Let go of me!"

For a moment he held on, looking down at her. The anger was still there, mixed with the surprise he had no way of knowing whether was because of their sudden appearance, or their appearance at all. And under it all, a touch of something it took him a moment to recognize through the rage.

Fear.

The moment the word formed in his mind, the moment he realized she was, in some way, afraid, he let go. It was instinctive, involuntary; it just wasn't in him to forcibly hold on to a frightened woman.

Crystal turned and ran, disappearing into one of the cottages closest to the garden shed, slamming the door behind her and, Gabe guessed, locking it.

"—guests of Miriam's, and we've seen Crystal's temper," Cara was saying soothingly to the man as Gabe turned that direction. He seemed calm enough now, although still a bit stunned at their unexpected intervention.

"I...thank you," he said. "I had no idea she could be violent. She caught me completely off guard."

He seemed to shake it off, and offered his hand to Gabe. "Mr. Taggert, I'm Lawrence Hammon. Miriam's son."

"Gabe, please," he said automatically.

The man looked to be in his mid-thirties, maybe a little older, and other than the golden brown eyes, he saw little resemblance to their hostess. Lawrence Hammon was taller than Cara, who was a tall woman, but shorter than his own six-one. He had the pale complexion of someone who spent most of his time inside. Worked in an office, Gabe guessed. His hair, lighter than his mother's, was longer than his own, but neatly styled, if a little thin on top.

"Mom told me she had some guests. I'm sorry we had to meet this way."

He glanced off in the direction Crystal had gone, frowning. Gabe could see the resemblance to Miriam now, more in profile than head-on. The nose, and chin, and when he turned back, it was there in the gentle smile.

"I worry about her," he said, and Gabe knew he wasn't talking about Crystal. "She's always taking in strays like that, thinking she can help."

"Maybe she does help," Cara said.

His brows furrowed again. "I'm not sure that one can be helped," he said frankly. "I get up here as often as I can, but I can't be here all the time. I wish Mom would move back down to civilization."

"I can see why she loves it here," Cara said, her tone a bit cautious, as if she didn't want to tread on any toes.

"She could come up here any time, I'd make sure of that. But I hate worrying about her here all alone, so far from help if she needed it."

Gabe could see his point, although Miriam certainly seemed healthy enough. He sympathized; he couldn't imagine what it must feel like. The admiral was hale and hearty and indomitable at sixty-one, and foolish though it was, Gabe couldn't picture him any other way. He supposed Miriam's son was worried about injury more than illness.

And after what they had just interrupted, Gabe didn't think Crystal's presence was of much comfort to him.

"So what was that all about?" he asked, indicating Crystal's cottage.

Lawrence frowned again. He hesitated, as if uncertain he should discuss it with strangers. Gabe guessed that their intervention, saving him from possible injury, decided him.

"I'm afraid she's been stealing again. Some valuable antique watches that belonged to my grandfather are missing. She says she doesn't know anything about it." He grimaced. "That was just before she took that swing at me."

"She's an angry young woman," Gabe said.

"Very," Lawrence agreed somewhat urgently.

"Are you going to report it?" Cara asked.

Lawrence blinked. "What?"

"It was an assault," Gabe pointed out. "If you want her out of here, I'm sure calling the sheriff would help."

"Oh. Yes." He'd obviously been more rattled than Gabe had realized by the near miss with the rake handle. Then he brightened, smiled at them. "And I have witnesses, don't I? My two Good Samaritans."

Cara smiled back, and Gabe couldn't help noting the appreciation that came into Lawrence's face as he looked at her.

Lawrence glanced toward the cottage again. "I don't know. If it were just me, I would, of course. But it would hurt my mother…she's so certain she can save that woman." He sighed. "I'll have to think about it."

Gabe's cell phone rang. As he pulled it out of his pocket, Lawrence excused himself, saying he was going inside to talk to his mother. Cara stood watching him go as Gabe glanced at his phone. The caller ID screen told him it was St. John, and he answered accordingly.

"Taggert."

"Airport, east end of the lake. Meet the Redstone chopper at Callahan Aviation. One hour."

Gabe opened his mouth to ask for details, remembered who he was talking to, and stopped himself. "Got it," he said instead.

"Anything else?"

"Not at the moment." Then, because, based on St. John's reputation, he knew the man who was both legend and mystery at Redstone was still digging, he added, "Our woman with the alias took a swing at somebody with a rake handle when he accused her of stealing from her benefactor."

"Touchy."

"Very."

"True?"

"Don't know. Wouldn't surprise me."

"You?"

It took Gabe a moment. "No, the son of the woman we're here to see."

"Name?"

"Lawrence Hammon," Gabe said, starting to feel a bit like a billiard ball in play.

"Be in touch."

The conversation ended on that, leaving Gabe a little unsure whether the last had been a promise or a request. He shook his head.

"A challenge, as always?" Cara asked.

She was smiling at him. Much more warmly than she'd smiled at Lawrence. He felt a bit like a high school kid the moment the assessment formed in his mind, but he couldn't seem to help it. He smiled back.

"As always," he agreed.

"I'd like to meet him someday," she said. "Just for the experience."

"It is one," he said. And quashed the sudden image that hit him, of introducing her to St. John and everyone else at Redstone. Quashed it because in his imagination, which had recently become annoyingly overactive, he was introducing her as *his*.

"We have an hour to get to the airport at the east end of the lake," he said, his tone sharper than he'd intended in his effort to control his own thoughts.

She glanced at the main building, where Lawrence had gone inside to speak to his mother. "I suppose our little experiment was inconclusive, given the circumstances."

"Afraid so."

With a nod, she turned and started to walk back the way they came, toward the car. She didn't speak again until they were outside the gate once more.

"So why are we going to the airport?"

"To meet the Redstone helicopter."

She took that in stride, merely lifting a brow. "Because?"

"I have no idea," Gabe said.

She laughed at his wry tone. "And that bothers you?"

"It doesn't you?" he countered.

"It would have, once," she admitted. "I liked having everything planned out, knowing what was going to happen and when."

Just the way he liked things, he thought. *Or always had.* He'd learned to let up on it a little, since he'd left the service. But it was still in his nature, and he didn't know if he could change it much more.

"Why'd you change?" he asked, genuinely curious.

"Hope," she said simply. "Life's too uncertain to miss out on things that could be wonderful just because it wasn't in your plans."

The uncomplicated truth of that hit him like Crystal's rake handle. He was vaguely aware that Hope had tried to tell him just that, in some form, many times. But he hadn't listened. Or at least, he hadn't heard. Hadn't understood. But now.

Was it that Hope wasn't here to say it that made it register now, when it never had before?

Or was it that Cara was?

He wrestled silently with both the idea and his guilt about his own response to it, throughout the drive to the airport. The GPS system had quickly given them directions to the mountain airport, about fifteen miles away. He shut off the voice commands; he didn't want them intruding. On what, he wasn't quite sure, since he seemed incapable of conversation at the moment.

And Cara didn't seem to mind. Unlike Hope, she apparently didn't feel the need to fill the silence with chatter. He'd learned to tune it out, sometimes to his detriment, such as when Hope had realized he wasn't paying attention and threw in something about an encounter with aliens that he hadn't noticed.

No, there were many things about Cara that were different. He'd always assumed it had been Cara who had gravitated to the outgoing, vivacious Hope, basking in the reflected glow, as it were. But now...now he was beginning think it might have been the other way around as well, that Hope might have needed Cara just as much, or even more. Cara was the kind of person you could always count on, a solid, steady, unwavering center that the brilliant star Hope could orbit around.

As they skirted the north shore of the lake, catching impressive vistas through the trees whenever the landscape would allow, he nearly snorted aloud at his own ridiculous musings. But the image wouldn't leave him, and he couldn't seem to stop himself from wondering what it would be like to have that solid, steady, unwavering center for himself.

Get your head out of the ozone, Taggert, he ordered silently. *Don't drive right past the damned airport.*

And yet again he wondered what the hell had happened to his vaunted ability to focus.

Chapter 18

Gabe seemed distracted, as he had most of the drive, and Cara was about to point out the sign that indicated the airport was to their right when he spotted it himself and made the turn they needed.

The airport was small, a single runway aimed directly at the easternmost point of the lake. That made it easy to find Callahan Aviation Services, although the moment she saw the gleaming, red and gray helicopter she guessed they were in the right place.

The burly, jovial man who greeted them introduced himself as George Callahan. He had known Josh, he told them, since he'd been just a lanky kid with a drawl and a dream.

"Your chariot awaits," he said with a laugh, gesturing toward the chopper before he left them. "And your pilot. Couldn't believe it when a woman got out. Not many female chopper pilots. But if Josh says she's good, then she's good. That thing came in and set down like a feather."

He apologized then for not being able to stick around, but he had a plane to ferry to an airport down on the flat for some repairs to the fuselage that they weren't equipped to handle.

"'Down on the flat' seems to be the term for it up here," Cara remarked as they walked toward the helicopter.

"I noticed," Gabe said.

As they neared the sleek craft glistening in the early spring sun, a figure walked out from behind it. Wearing the red shirt with the Redstone logo like Gabe had had on, but with unmistakably female curves, the woman was a couple of inches shorter than her own five-nine, with dark hair in a short, tousled cut that seemed to emphasize huge, dark eyes. Her bone structure was exquisite, with high cheekbones that gave her a stunning, slightly exotic look.

Then she smiled as she spotted them, and even from thirty feet away Cara felt the warmth of it. She gestured over, and they kept walking.

"Tess Machado," Gabe murmured.

"You know her?" Cara asked.

"Of her," Gabe said. "She's a legend at Redstone. Been there longer than almost anyone. She's Josh's personal pilot."

"I thought he was his own pilot."

"He was, up until a few years ago. Now most of the time he has too much to do, and needs to work in flight. She's the only one he'll surrender the controls to."

Impressed, Cara looked at the woman with respect. And with an instinctive liking; that smile was killer. She wondered how old Tess was; maybe late-thirties, although Cara guessed she'd look much the same twenty years from now.

The brief introductions corroborated Gabe's guess about her identity.

"I've heard of you," Gabe told the woman.

"Back at you," Tess said, the smile widening. "How's that sweet new boat?"

"Sweet," Gabe confirmed with an answering smile. He glanced at the chopper. "Not the same one you flew out of Colombia under fire, I hope?"

Cara smothered a gasp. Under fire? But Tess merely lifted a brow at him. "Heard about that, huh?"

"All of Redstone's heard about that," he said. "You don't rescue the head of security and Redstone's chief point man through a hail of gunfire without word getting around."

She shrugged, as if it were all in a day's work. There was, Cara thought, more to working for Redstone than she'd ever realized.

"You're safe," she said, the smile becoming a grin. "Different bird."

"Does Mr. Redstone design helicopters, too?" Cara asked.

"No," Tess said. "About the only thing he doesn't."

There was admiration, respect, and something more in the woman's voice.

"Yet," Gabe said, and Tess laughed.

"Good point," she said. Then the smile disappeared as she looked at them seriously. "I know this isn't going to be pleasant for either of you. I hope we're able to help put this to rest once and for all."

"Thank you," Cara said, meaning it.

"Let's go. Ryan Barton's already on board. Redstone tech-head," she explained. She said it with respect, not mockery, Cara noted.

"St. John sent a tech guy?" Gabe asked.

Tess nodded. "With Ian Gamble's latest invention."

Cara sensed Gabe react to the name. She glanced at him. "Redstone's resident genius inventor," Gabe said.

"He is that," Tess agreed. "You want anything from a prosthetic foot that responds like you were born with it, to an explosive-sensitive paint, Ian's your guy."

The range of those ideas left Cara a little stunned as they headed toward the helicopter. It was much bigger than it had appeared to her at first, and she couldn't help feeling a bit nervous.

"Never been in an egg-beater before?" Tess asked cheerfully.

"No," Cara admitted. "I try to stay away from machines that seemed designed to tear themselves apart."

Tess laughed, a genuine, warm laugh that made Cara smile despite her unease.

"The opposite, actually," she said. "It's the design that keeps them from tearing themselves apart."

As long as nothing breaks, Cara thought, but didn't voice the words. But if this woman had done what Gabe had said, rescued two people out of some Colombian jungle or wherever, with people shooting at them, she could no doubt handle something as routine as this.

"Get seasick?" Tess asked.

"No," Cara said.

"Then you should be fine," Tess said blithely.

Cara wasn't so sure, but she didn't see that she had much choice at the moment; she let Tess lead the way to the door of the waiting aircraft.

"Just what is this new invention?" Cara asked as she climbed aboard. Gabe, she noted, didn't wait and let Tess board before him. Some captain-of-the-ship last protocol? she wondered.

"I'll let Ryan explain," Tess said when she'd joined them. She glanced toward the front of the craft, where Cara guessed a co-pilot would sit if there was one. A young man with short, spiky hair bleached blond at the ends sat checking the stability of a large, complicated-looking device that appeared to be bolted to the helicopter's floor, if that's what it was called.

"In terms we can all understand," Tess added with a grin at the young man.

He smiled back at her. Cara imagined it would be hard for anyone not to.

"It's a pulse induction metal detector," Ryan said without bothering to introduce himself. Apparently he assumed Tess had already handled that, or it wasn't worth his time; he was obviously focused on the machine before him. "It's pretty standard for the most part, really. It fires a high-voltage pulse, and measures the time it takes for the voltage to drop into the target. If there's metal, it takes longer."

"For the most part?" Gabe asked.

The smile widened. "Well, it *is* a Gamble variation. What Mr.

Gamble did was amazing. He came up with a way to amplify and narrow the pulse so it could be used at a distance. Usually you have to be right on the ground for a metal detector to work."

Gabe's brows rose. "An airborne metal detector?"

"Yep." The young tech looked as excited as if he'd invented the thing himself. "And it's tied into a GPS system, so that if you can't land in the vicinity, people on the ground can find the exact spot. He's still fine-tuning it. It won't find small things yet, only things bigger than, say, a lawnmower, but something like a car? Easy."

"Ryan," Tess said softly. The young man looked at her, then colored fiercely. Cara guessed he'd just remembered exactly why they were looking for a car, and what else they might find if they located Hope's.

"I'm sorry. I get sort of excited."

"It's all right," Cara said, putting a hand on the boy's—he seemed like one to her now—arm.

"I hope you're still as enthused after we've found a dozen or so but not the one we're looking for," Gabe said, his casual tone easing the boy's discomfiture.

"We'll find it," Ryan promised.

"Yes," Gabe said with a level, quiet determination. "If I have to check every chunk of metal bigger than a lawnmower in these mountains."

"We," Cara said softly.

Gabe looked at her then, and some of the grimness faded from his eyes. "Yes," he said simply, and Cara felt a tightening in her chest when he didn't dispute her. They took their seats behind Tess and Ryan, and Cara spent a long moment fussing with the harness that seemed ominously more complicated than an airplane seat belt. Finally Gabe helped her, and she wondered if he'd logged some hours in navy choppers.

An hour later, she was wondering if perhaps Tess had been a bit optimistic in her prediction that Cara would be fine. She'd never been on a ride like this one. No roller coaster or thrill ride could ever have prepared her for this. The chopper lifted, dived, hovered, and sometimes seemed to spin in place, with a swift nimbleness that took her breath away and more than once sent her stomach plummeting.

And Tess Machado did it all without fuss, with a smooth, casual ease that Cara marveled at even as she fought the occasional blip of motion-induced nausea. Cara had given up trying to figure out how the thing worked; all she was sure of was that it took both hands and both feet, working in concert in a way that only increased the admiration she already felt for the woman. She tried to tell herself it was like driving a car, it became automatic after a while, but she wasn't convinced.

Despite her seeming complete focus on the controls—two foot pedals and two hand controls she called the collective and the cyclic—Tess noticed Cara's scrutiny.

"Somebody," Tess said, her voice coming clearly through the pair of headphones she'd given them all, "once said flying a helicopter was like standing on a greased beach ball while playing the drums."

Cara laughed, and her nervousness eased. "Where did you learn?"

"Josh taught me."

"Himself?" Gabe asked, hearing the conversation on his own headset.

"Yes. He said there were Redstone operations in places a fixed-wing couldn't get to, so I'd better learn."

"You obviously took to it," Gabe said.

"I can fly," she said simply.

Cara thought about that while Ryan interrupted, directing Tess toward something he'd seen on the screen. The words were just that, simple, but the world of quiet confidence behind them made her smile, and want to get to know this remarkable woman better.

Tess followed Ryan's directions, as she had three times already, bringing the chopper down low enough that Cara felt her heart start to hammer all over again. Even she, who knew nothing about helicopters, could see that this was some tricky flying in narrow, dangerous quarters. Yet Tess never turned a hair, just did it, brought them in close, and this time as once before, let the rotor wash part the trees they hovered over enough for them to see that this time, unlike last time when it had been an abandoned tractor, it was indeed a car.

It was not, however, Hope's little red coupe.

They lifted away.

"You're marking these, right, Ryan?" Tess asked. "We'll turn it over to the sheriff's office when we're done. They can check them out, make sure there's no one else going through this unnecessarily."

Cara went still. "I...hadn't thought. I'm glad you're doing that."

"It's the Redstone way," she replied.

Cara glanced at Gabe. He smiled at her, his expression confirming Tess's simple declaration. And Cara realized then that, even if he missed the navy, Gabe was happy where he was. And that eased a pain she hadn't even realized she was carrying.

A few minutes later they again followed Ryan's directions. They made a note of the location when Tess finally announced the power lines nearby made it impossible for them to get close enough; they'd check that later from the ground if necessary.

By the time they were heading up a small ravine near where Gabe had said would be his pick, Cara was thinking she might almost be getting used to this. Then Ryan spoke, and before she could brace herself the bottom dropped out again.

Nope, she thought. *No way I'll get used to this.*

But at least she hadn't humiliated herself by having to reach for the airsickness bag Tess had discreetly and kindly pointed out to her. *Yet,* although if this kept up—

Her thoughts cut off as Gabe went rigid beside her. Tess dropped down a little farther, trees whipping beneath them. And finally, as she followed Gabe's gaze instead of looking randomly, she saw it.

A flash of red at the bottom of the ravine.

"Tess," Gabe said, his voice tense.

"Got it," Tess said.

And, impossibly, they dropped farther. Cara would have sworn they were going to hit the trees and go careening down the mountainside. But Tess held them rock-steady as Gabe leaned forward, at his eyes a pair of binoculars Tess had retrieved for him before they'd taken off.

"It's oxidized a lot, but I think it's the right color," Gabe said. "Size looks right. Can you give me a bit to your right?"

"A bit," Tess said. And the helicopter obediently shifted. The wind of their presence gave them a slightly better look. Cara's pulse was racing now as she peered at the obviously battered vehicle below.

"It didn't burn," Gabe whispered.

Cara's breath caught; she hadn't allowed herself to consider any details, but now that he'd said it the possibilities flooded in. At first she was relieved, but what if Hope had been injured, and had lain helpless and in pain, what if—

She felt Gabe's hand on hers.

"Don't," he said. "We don't even know yet."

She suppressed a shudder, but with a strength he seemed to have loaned her, fought down the images.

"We're not going to land just yet," Tess said on the intercom, sounding regretful. "No place even close to set down."

"I've got the coordinates," Ryan said.

Tess took over then, as if she sensed both Cara and Gabe were too shell-shocked. Cara vaguely heard her giving the information to someone and instructing them to call the sheriff's office. Heard her say this was positive enough they were going to suspend the search awaiting confirmation. Heard her tell them to use all the weight the Redstone name could bring to bear to get them moving quickly.

Through all of it Cara sat strapped in the helicopter's passenger seat, trying not to think. But somewhere, deep inside, in the part of her heart that had always belonged to her dearest friend, she knew.

They'd found Hope.

And now they would know for sure that they'd lost her forever.

Chapter 19

After the initial reaction, Gabe thought, it was all oddly anti-climactic. As if finding Hope had merely put the period at the end of a tragic story already read. Still sad, still painful, but inevitable.

Because he was sure. Just as Cara was; he could see it in her eyes.

They had gone back to the airport, setting down at Callahan's and taking up residence in the comfortable lounge Mrs. Callahan showed them to.

"Any friend of Josh's is a friend of ours," she declared, and proceeded to brew up a fresh pot of coffee for them.

A while later, after having seen to the care and feeding of her aircraft, Tess joined them. Ryan, she said, was still aboard, processing the data they'd gathered on other vehicles to turn over to the authorities.

"St. John will get the call, and he'll call me," she said. "I gave the job to him. He's the best at exerting Redstone pressure if necessary."

"I can imagine," Gabe said.

"What's his story?" Cara asked, as if looking for distraction. Gabe listened curiously himself, figuring Tess, being so close to Josh and having been with Redstone for so long, would know if anyone did.

She didn't.

"Not a clue. I mean, I know the basics, that he's been with Josh nearly since the beginning, that he's actually known him since childhood. Longer than any of us, really, even me and John Draven, who have been with Redstone the longest."

"No idea why he's...." She stopped, and Gabe knew she didn't want to insult the man who was doing so much to help them.

"The way he is?" Tess asked with a smile. "No. Rumors abound, but the truth? Only he and Josh know for sure, I'd guess. Maybe not even Josh knows it all."

Gabe listened as the two women talked, although he wasn't fully tuned in. He noted they seemed to find a lot in common, including a shared interest in reading—in particular, they both admitted with a grin, mysteries and thrillers.

Time ticked on, an hour, then two, and as the twilight started to deepen Gabe barely managed to restrain himself from pacing. Soon it would be too dark, if it wasn't already in that deep ravine. If they didn't get there and report back soon, it would be tomorrow before they knew.

As if she'd sensed his edginess, Tess tried to draw him into the conversation.

"So what's your passion, besides the sea?" she asked.

It was all Gabe could do to keep from looking over at Cara. He chewed on himself a little, asking what the hell he was doing thinking about Cara and passion and the inevitable scenarios that juxtaposition put in his head, when they likely had just found his dead wife.

"I always thought about learning to fly," he said, almost desperately, figuring that would get Tess going. It did. And saved him from his own thoughts as well, as he and Tess settled into a pilot-to-pilot discussion of the differences. and similarities between ships of the sea and the air, finding more in common than he would have expected. Cara listened with every evidence of interest.

"Flying this high in the mountains is different," Tess said. "The winds can be really tricky. Those ridges at the north end of the airfield can really keep things stirred up."

"Wind shear?" Gabe asked.

She nodded. "Fortunately it's pretty calm today. And cool, so density altitude isn't an issue."

"Density altitude?" Cara asked.

"When it's warm, like in the summer up here, the air mass expands, the molecules moving farther apart. Makes the air thinner, and flying in it an interesting thing."

"Both helicopter and fixed-wing?" Gabe asked.

She nodded. "Different, obviously, but—"

She stopped as her cell phone rang. All three of them froze, and no matter how Gabe tried to tell himself it could be anyone calling her, he knew it wasn't. And when she looked at the caller ID screen a second more than was necessary, he knew he was right. He saw that Cara knew, too; she rose and walked over to the window, looking out at the airfield as if turning her back on what was happening could stop it.

"Machado." A pause. "Yes, they're here." Another, even briefer pause, telling Gabe it was likely St. John himself. "All right. Any details?"

After another brief pause she, as had St. John no doubt, hung up without another word. Gabe read the news in her face before she said gently, "It's confirmed. The license plate matches, and…there are human remains."

Cara made a tiny sound that wrenched at him. He couldn't stop himself from going to her. She turned and came into his arms without hesitation, leaned against him, and he felt the quiver that went through her.

Tess spoke again, in the manner of someone wanting to get

it all said fast. "They're recovering everything. It will take some time to get the car out, but…the body is already on its way to the county morgue below. They know what happened with your car, so they'll be looking very carefully. He'll call with anything new."

Gabe nodded. Tess whispered, "I'm sorry. Both of you."

"Thank you," Cara said, her voice breaking between the words. Tess nodded, turned and silently left the room.

Gabe just stood there, holding her, unexpectedly finding comfort of his own in the gesture he'd meant to give to her. He felt another quiver, then another, then realized she was crying. He opened his mouth to say something, anything, then shut it again, thinking there was nothing to say, not really.

The quiet weeping eased sooner than he'd expected. But then, Cara hadn't been what he'd expected from the moment she'd walked back into his life.

"I thought I was prepared," she said. "It's been so long, she's been missing from my life for so long, I didn't think it would hit me so hard."

"That doesn't mean it still isn't a shock," he said. "I've known for a long time something like this was probably the answer, but…."

"I thought I'd just feel…at peace," she said. "To finally know, for sure."

"It will come," he said, wishing he believed it.

"I know," she said, as if she did. "But right now, it's hard."

"Yes," he agreed. And kept holding her.

They stood together to watch Tess take off into the darkness, flashing red lights the only thing they could see to tell them where the sleek chopper was. Then the bright headlight swept over them as the bird lifted and turned practically on an axis, and wind swept over them as it soared into the night.

"I like her," Cara said.

"Me, too. I can see why Josh relies on her."

It was a moment before she asked him, "Now what?"

He let out a compressed breath. "Until we hear if there's any evidence of tampering, I'm not sure there's anything we can do but wait."

"And tell Miriam," she said softly.

"Yes." His reluctance was clear, but she knew he wouldn't shirk the task.

"Shall we go back there now?"

"Might as well," he said. "Get it over with."

They talked little on the drive, each absorbed in their own memories of the golden girl they'd both loved, and both lost. When they arrived back at the inn, Cara noticed Gabe set the alarm on the car, a simple action that still made her shiver.

Telling Miriam was difficult, as Cara had expected; they'd had eight years to expect this; Miriam had now learned Hope was missing and now dead within two days.

By tacit agreement they didn't mention Crystal; there didn't seem any point in adding their suspicions to her grief, not yet. And after a while, Miriam got out a bottle of a sweet almond liqueur Hope had liked, and poured them all enough to toast.

"To Hope, who touched us all, and will never be forgotten," she said simply.

The sound of their glasses clinking together seemed like a death knell to Cara, an audible acknowledgment of the truth they'd learned today. And when Miriam insisted it was far too late to drive down the mountain, they agreed, for her sake as much as theirs, to stay another night.

"Do we need to watch out for Crystal?" Gabe asked casually, as if he were only concerned with avoiding the cranky young woman.

Miriam frowned. "I don't know. She left this afternoon, and I haven't seen her." She sighed. "I'm afraid she and my son simply do not get along."

Cara just managed to stop herself from saying *Hard to believe*; sarcasm didn't seem appropriate just now.

"I'm sure Lawrence is just concerned about you," she said instead.

"Yes," Miriam agreed. "He always worries. But sometimes I have to remind him who's the parent."

Cara smiled at that.

Later, as they were going upstairs to their respective rooms, Gabe said thoughtfully, "Well, that's three of us who don't trust Miss Crystal."

"Yes," Cara said.

She opened the door to the green room, then turned back to say goodnight, only to find Gabe standing much closer than she'd realized. Something in his face, some shadow in his eyes as he looked down at her, made her instinctively reach for him, put her arms around him.

"I'm sorry, Gabe," she said quietly.

He said nothing, but after a moment his arms came around her in turn. For a long time they just stood there, taking comfort, warmth and support from each other.

When Gabe bent his head and pressed his lips to her forehead, her heart leaped at the contact.

Stop it, she ordered herself. *It's the kind of kiss you'd give your sister.*

With the idea of forcing herself to stop her own silly thoughts, she made herself look up at him, knowing she would see only the friendly concern she'd always seen in Gabriel Taggert's eyes. Knowing that would quash these impossible longings where nothing else could. She was just the old Cara to him, glamorous, glorious Hope's quiet, shy, studious friend, and she always would be.

What she saw in his eyes burned away all pretense.

Cara's heart slammed in her chest. Never in her life had she thought any man would look at her like this. As if she were the only water in a lifetime of thirst, as if she were the answer to prayers he'd never dared to pray.

That it was Gabe made her forget how to breathe.

She opened her mouth to speak, but no words came. There was only a niggling fear that if she spoke she would ruin this moment, and never, ever know if he really meant it.

Gabe made an odd sound, something like a groan that rumbled up from deep in his chest. He seemed to take her parted lips as invitation, and lowered his head.

The moment his mouth closed over hers, any idea she'd had that he looked at her as a sister vanished, seared to ash in the sudden heat. As did all the imaginings she'd ever had about what it would be like to be kissed by this man. As the girl she'd been, she'd had little to judge by. As the few men in her life had come and gone since, she'd told herself the fire she'd imagined had been only that, a girl's dream, that no reality could measure up to her imaginings about Gabe. She'd loved her fiancé, but that had been a quiet, solid thing. Not this. Not fire.

She'd been wrong. And right. Reality could measure up. But only if that reality was Gabe himself.

His arms tightened around her as he deepened the kiss, and the pressure as he tested the softness of her lips was somehow the most arousing thing she'd ever felt.

No, it was the taste of him, of his mouth, and the heat, the incredible heat of him.

No, she thought foggily then, it was the feel of him, of his tall, hard body against hers, not a fraction of space between them. That was the most arousing thing she'd ever felt.

A moan escaped her, a sound unlike anything she could ever recall making before. But she was helpless to stop it before the onslaught of sensations being unleashed in her.

The reality was definitely living up to the dream.

When at last he pulled back, she whimpered a protest, unable to form a coherent word.

"Cara," he whispered. "Stop me now."

For a moment she just stared at him. Why on earth would she want to stop him, when she'd dreamed of this for years?

"Why?" It was the only word she could manage.

"So many reasons," he said, but he didn't let go of her, and the feel of him swamped any vestige of rationality left in her brain. On some level she knew he was right, there were so many reasons she shouldn't do this.

"But only one reason matters to me," she said softly.

He went very still. "What?"

"I will regret it the rest of my life if we don't."

She meant it. She would forever regret if she didn't—even if it was just this once—find out what this man really meant to her.

He groaned, louder then, and his arms tightened around her. She heard a sound, realized with a little shock that somehow they were in her room and he'd shut the door behind them. And then she was up against that closed door, the raised panel digging into her back as his mouth closed hungrily over hers once more. And then she felt nothing but him. His mouth on hers. His hands on her, stroking, exploring, learning. And he did learn; despite the fact that she could barely think, he was learning every spot that made her gasp, every caress that made her quiver.

For a moment she thought of Hope, and guilt surged through her. But, oddly, the thought was of Hope complaining about Gabe's ability to compartmentalize, to focus on one endeavor to the exclusion of all else, while she, Hope, could only scatter her attention amid everything before her.

Cara's last rational thought was disbelief; how could Hope have ever complained when it meant this could happen? When it meant this kind of fierce, intense, single-minded attention, as if you were the only person who existed for him?

When it meant that he could make you feel that you were the absolute center of his world?

Any lingering idea that she would feel as if she were stealing something from her best friend turned to smoke when his hands found her breasts, cupped them, lifted. It took a moment for her dazed mind to realize she wasn't feeling his touch through layers of clothing. And she didn't care that he'd lifted her shirt, unclasped her bra to bare her for his caress, leaving her only with the gold chain with the carved, pale green jade initial *T* she wore—for Thorpe, she always said, although in her heart she'd often thought of Taggert as well—all with her being only faintly aware. Not only did she not care, but she found herself arching her back, pushing herself into his hands, offering in a way she'd never wanted to before.

Gabe swore, low and harsh. And then, in a move so effortless she nearly gasped, he swept her up in his arms and carried her to the bed with the sea-green comforter. With that same ruthless efficiency he stripped the rest of her clothes off, and Cara helped him with an urgency that would have embarrassed her with any other man.

He kicked off his shoes and yanked his own shirt over his head. Cara smothered a gasp; the thought had just hit her that she was about to have the chance to fulfill her imaginings, and follow that trail of dark, crisp hair downward.

He paused with his hands on the button of the black jeans that had so taunted her since he'd put them on.

"Stop me now, Cara," he said again, then added the ultimatum, "or never."

"I choose never," she said, before second thoughts could invade, before anything could interfere with the dream come true before her.

The sound he made then was more growl than groan, and he shed the rest of his clothes in a rush. She had a split second to realize he was even more beautiful than she'd imagined before he was beside her, and the feel of him pressed to her, skin to skin, sent her mind reeling and seemed to end her capacity for thought altogether.

He was everywhere, caressing her not only with his hands and that incredible mouth, but with his entire body, rubbing, stroking, until she was unable to do anything less than ripple beneath the assault on her senses. It went on and on, and she heard herself cry out again and again. With every touch she felt a wondrous, stunning clenching inside as need gripped her in a way she'd never known.

"Gabe," she whispered finally, desperately. "Please."

"I thought you'd never ask." His voice was gravel-rough and sent a shudder through her.

And then he was over her, reaching to guide himself as she opened for him, lifting her hips, wanting, needing this man inside her more than she needed to breathe. At the first probing touch she smothered a gasp. As he slid forward, his way eased by her own slick readiness, she cried out at the delicious stretching sensation.

He stopped. "Cara?"

She couldn't speak. Could only moan. She reached for him then, grasped his lean hips and urged him on without the words she couldn't seem to form.

He surged into her then, and she cried out anew with the glorious shock of feeling him deep and thick and hot inside her. For a moment they froze, as if in wonder at a sensation as old as time and yet a new discovery for them both.

And then, with a heartfelt, shuddering oath, Gabe began to move, slow at first, and then faster, until Cara thought she would die from the sweet friction. She savored every involuntary sound he made, every shiver that went through him. And then, when he shifted his position slightly and she felt his body stroke hers in that swollen, critical spot, she gave up her grip on awareness and clung to him as the pressure built unbearably.

And then he said her name on a gasp, slammed into her hard and deep, and she cried out his name in turn as the hot, pulsing convulsions took her.

And she knew that, for once, it was the dream that didn't live up to the reality.

Chapter 20

The ring of his cell phone brought Gabe out of the soundest sleep he'd had in recent memory. That abrupt awakening was followed by the equally jolting realization that he wasn't alone. He was in bed, naked, wrapped around the equally naked but much softer and lovelier Cara Thorpe.

Some part of his mind that wasn't numbed by that shock was registering the number of rings, and considering where his phone was—in the pocket of the jeans that were several feet away on the floor—he calculated he wasn't going to get there before it went to voice mail, so he didn't even try. He wasn't sure he could move anyway.

He was in bed with his wife's best friend.

"Phone's ringing," that friend said sleepily.

"It'll stop," he said, wondering if he sounded as gruff to her as he did to himself.

For a moment it didn't matter that Hope was gone, had been gone for eight years.

Dead, he reminded himself grimly. There was no longer any doubt about that. He didn't need the coroner's ID to tell him; he knew in his gut, had known since the moment he'd seen that flash of faded red through the trees in that ravine.

The phone did indeed stop ringing. Nothing else changed. His wife was dead, and he was in bed with her best friend. Not only in bed with her, but becoming aroused all over again at the memories of the night they'd just spent, spent with a passion he hadn't thought himself capable of anymore. The first time had been amazing enough. But when he'd awakened some hours later wanting, needing more, she hadn't protested when his touch disturbed her sleep; instead she'd turned to him willingly, welcomingly, and it had been even more incredible.

But nothing had been as incredible as the moment when her soft, curious touch had awakened him, and the thought that shy little Cara wanted him enough to wake him from sleep had been the most potent of aphrodisiacs.

He was pretty sure he'd shouted her name that time.

His phone chirped, the announcement that he had voice mail. The slant of sunlight through the window told him it was later than he was used to sleeping. He'd taken off his watch, not wanting to risk scratching her silken skin, and there was no clock on the bedside table as there was in his room.

No, there was, he realized as he glanced that way, she'd just turned it away.

Now that was something he couldn't understand. If he woke up in the night, that was the first thing he did, check the time. It was instinctive, natural, he thought, and he didn't quite understand how you could not want to know what time it was.

"You're frowning," she said, and he realized she'd come fully awake and was looking at him. And he felt her retreat from him, even though she moved only slightly in his arms.

"Was I?"

She lowered her eyes, and he thought he felt a tiny sigh escape her. "I was afraid you'd regret this."

It took him a moment to understand what she meant. Before he could speak, she went on softly.

"I understand. It's Hope. She'll always be there, won't she." It wasn't a question. And then her gaze came back to his face. "I don't regret it, Gabe. I can't. But I understand how you feel, really."

"I'm not sure I do," Gabe said honestly. "But that wasn't what I was frowning about. I was trying to figure out what happened to the clock."

She blinked. "The clock?" Then her expression cleared. "Oh. The clock."

Clearly she wasn't at her usual peak first thing in the morning, Gabe thought. He was telling himself he'd have to remember that before he realized the implications of what he was thinking.

"I turned it because it's very bright," she said. "It was annoying."

He felt oddly relieved at that. And that, plus the knowledge that he'd been thinking he would even need to remember she woke up more slowly than he did, was unsettling enough to drive him out of bed and over to the phone that had just chirped again.

He dragged the jeans back on before he pulled the phone out of his pocket. It was time for some fresh clothes, he thought as he pushed the appropriate button, glad he'd grabbed socks and that pair of boxers in the little store, even if they were a rather startling shade of St. Patrick's Day green.

He sensed Cara getting up, but didn't look at her. Didn't dare; if he got a glimpse of that lithe, lusciously curved body in the morning sun, he was liable to swoop down on her and take her right back to bed. Not something he wanted to do before he had a chance to think about what had happened between them. To figure out if he'd made one of the bigger mistakes of his life last night.

If it had been any other woman, he wouldn't be lost in this quagmire of confusion. But it wasn't. It was Cara.

As he zipped the jeans he wondered a little that she hadn't complained at all—Hope would have been frantic—about heading into the third day in the same clothes. Although he'd never have known it to look at them. He'd noticed yesterday morning that she'd washed her underwear; it had been hard to miss the silky bikini panties and matching, lace-trimmed bra hung over the shower enclosure, even if she hadn't blushingly apologized for the "extra décor" when she'd later found them where he'd laid them on the counter to keep them from getting wet from his shower.

She disappeared into the bathroom while he worked his way through the voice mail menu. He hadn't told her, of course, about the effect those intimate articles had had on him. Not, he thought as he remembered last night's fierce passion again, that it would come as any surprise to her now.

He finally got to the actual message. He listened, at first mildly amused by the fact that St. John was reading something to him, and therefore actually using complete sentences. But his amusement faded quickly, and when he disconnected he saw that Cara was back, wrapped in a bath towel, looking at him.

"St. John," he said. "Speaking in full sentences, for once."

Her brows rose. "Why?"

"He was reading the preliminary report from the first-glance inspection of the car."

She said nothing, just waited; obviously she'd accepted that Redstone got results fast, even from law enforcement. He recited what St. John had said, the words already etched deep into his mind.

"They said that the deterioration after all this time was severe, but the car had landed at an angle that had somewhat protected the undercarriage. It will take closer scrutiny in the lab to be sure, but they think there are tool marks near where a brake line would have been secured to the frame."

She got to it as quickly as he had. "It was no accident."

"Any more than ours would have been."

Cara drew herself up then. Any semblance of sleepiness had vanished. Her eyes seemed to have turned an even more vivid blue as her gaze narrowed. A fierce anger seemed to radiate from her, and even wrapped in just a bath towel, with her copper hair tousled around her head, she looked suddenly more like an avenging angel than the soft, eager woman whose slick heat had taken him in and sent him flying.

"Crystal," she said.

"And her clippers," Gabe agreed.

"Coincidence?"

"That she was here both times? That she carries those things like some women carry a lipstick? And that she's a snarly, short-tempered, angry—"

He stopped when Cara held up a hand. "I get it."

"I don't believe in that much coincidence."

"Nor do I."

"But why?" Cara asked. "Hope would have been kind to her, as kind as Miriam. You know she would, she wanted everyone to like her."

He'd been thinking about this since long before he'd heard what the sheriff's office had found. "Maybe Miriam is the key."

Cara thought about that for a moment before nodding slowly as she said, "I've noticed that, for all her nastiness, Crystal seems almost…protective of her. Maybe she was afraid Hope would be competition for Miriam's help and attention."

He hadn't thought of it in exactly that way, but now that Cara had put it into words, it had the ring of logic.

"She had a cushy nest here, and she thought Hope threatened that for some reason."

"Because," Cara said slowly, thoughtfully, "Hope and Miriam had something in common that Crystal could never share."

"The writing," Gabe said instantly.

Cara nodded.

"It's still just speculation," Gabe warned her.

"I know. But it makes sense, doesn't it?"

"Perfectly."

"Do we tell the sheriff?"

"We do," Gabe said. "But I'm not about to leave it to when-ever they can get to it. Especially knowing they likely can't make a move until they have the final report on the possible tampering."

"Let's go," she said abruptly, turning back into the bathroom.

"Go?"

"Find Crystal," she said, as if it were obvious. Since that was exactly what he'd planned on, he supposed it was.

"Let me handle this, Cara."

She turned back. "What?"

"If she did this, she could be dangerous."

The anger that had ebbed slightly flared in her eyes once more. "I'm in this, Gabriel Taggert. It's why I'm here. Don't think because of that—" she gestured toward the bed and its tangled, tossed covers "—you get to order me around."

He opened his mouth to say that had nothing to do with it, but he wasn't sure it was true so bit back the words. "'That?'" he quoted back instead.

With a look of pure exasperation she put her hands on her hips—those beautiful, womanly hips he'd had his own hands on not so long ago, as he'd pulled her atop him for a ride unlike anything he'd ever felt before—and glared at him.

"It's time to finish this, for Hope. We can talk about *that* later."

She closed the bathroom door in his face. He had no doubt she had used the word again simply to prod him. And once again he realized Cara Thorpe was unlike any woman he'd known. He couldn't think of one he'd ever been intimate with who wouldn't have wanted to dissect what had happened between them down to the last detail.

He gathered up the rest of his clothes and darted, half-dressed, back to the blue room.

Retreated, you mean.

This time, despite the situation they were in, the little voice in his head made him smile.

When did you turn into such a bitch? Cara asked herself. The guy was just trying to protect you. It's who he is, what he does.

But she couldn't be left out of this. After eight years they were close, so close to finding out exactly what had happened to Hope, and there was no way she was going to sit on the sidelines.

She gave herself a little shake, and with no small effort managed not to look at her tangled bed while she considered her clothing options. The T-shirt she'd slept in was wrinkled, but in better shape than the green blouse she'd been wearing.

And of course, she hadn't worn it last night, she thought wryly as she lost the battle for a moment and looked at the bed where she'd learned she really knew very little of how things could be with the right—or in this case, likely very wrong—man.

A shiver went through her at the memory. She made herself move.

She rolled up her blouse and put it in the bag from the general store. She'd like to steam the wrinkles out of the T-shirt, as she had with her blouse and pants yesterday, but Gabe was in the shower now and there was no way she was going in there. That she had the implied right, after the night they'd spent, and that she wouldn't see anything she hadn't already explored with great detail and delight, was something she tried not to dwell on.

She pulled on the T-shirt. Body heat would smooth it out a bit, she told herself, then groaned inwardly at her own choice of words.

Body heat, indeed.

Miriam was in the kitchen when they got downstairs. Her expression was rather bleak, but she gave them a smile anyway. And handed them a folder full of printed pages.

"I couldn't sleep, so I went back and pulled up Hope's letters and the rest of the stories she sent me. I thought you might like to have them."

"Thank you, Miriam," Cara said, reaching out to touch the older woman's hand.

"Yes," Gabe said, his voice suspiciously tight, as if the single syllable was all he trusted himself to say.

"Where's Crystal this morning?" Cara asked. "I hope she'll be here to keep you company after we leave."

Gabe went still, as if he hadn't expected her to jump right into today's order of business, but Cara didn't see any point in wasting time. She felt a little guilty not telling Miriam the truth, but on the slim chance they were wrong, she didn't want to hurt the woman's feelings unnecessarily.

"She'll be back later. She went down to the store in town, to get...some hardware thing she needed, I forget. But Lawrence is still here. He was going to leave last night, but decided to stay when he heard the news. He knew I was upset."

Cara wondered where he'd stayed, since Miriam had indicated the two rooms they'd been using—well, one last night, she amended silently, fighting the heat that threatened once more— were the only ones kept ready for guests inside the main building.

"I'm sorry if we evicted him from his usual room."

"He prefers one of the cottages, actually. He's sleeping late, as usual, I'm afraid."

Cara glanced at Gabe. "I'm not sure who put the morning people in charge, and Lawrence has my empathy."

One corner of Gabe's mouth twitched upward. "No sense waiting until the day's half-gone to get started," he said mildly.

"Hmpf," Cara said.

They waited for a while, forgoing Miriam's offer of another full breakfast and sitting down instead with some English muffins and coffee, but Crystal didn't return. Finally Cara looked up at Gabe, and saw he was thinking the same thing she was, that Crystal had taken to her heels for good, once she'd learned Hope's body had been found.

Eventually they said goodbye to Miriam, who elicited a promise from them that they would keep her apprised and come back to visit. They walked out to the car, where Gabe proceeded to go over it inch by inch, top and bottom, looking for any sign of tampering.

"Nothing," he said finally, sliding out from under the car and getting up off the ground, dusting off what he could of the debris his clothes had collected. Instinctively she moved to help, brushing pine needles off his shoulders and studiously avoiding those that were clinging to his temptingly muscled backside.

"Thanks," he said when she stepped back, and the husky note that had come into his voice reminded her of how he'd sounded in the dark. Which reminded her of how he'd felt in the dark. How he'd made her feel.

The heat rose yet again, and she spoke quickly. "I suppose we should check around in town, just in case she's really there."

"Yes. If we don't find her, I'd say we call the sheriff's office, tell them Crystal may have taken off. Might be enough to tip them into seriously considering her a suspect."

Cara nodded in agreement.

"But first," Gabe said, "I think I'll call St. John. See if there's anything in the facts he dug up that might indicate where she'd go."

They got into the car, and since he was driving he used the hands-free system as they started down the mountain. Or perhaps it was just as much so that she could hear, and he wouldn't have to repeat everything.

Not that there was much to repeat, given he was talking to St. John.

After the amazingly short conversation about checking into where Crystal might run to, St. John changed the subject. To one even less pleasant.

"Prelim from the coroner. Want it?"

Cara went still. Gabe glanced at her, and she read in his face that he would tell St. John to hold it for him, if she didn't want to hear it. And she didn't, God help her, she didn't. But she had to. She had to as much as Gabe had to. She gave a short, sharp nod.

"Go ahead," Gabe said, his voice flat.

"Broken neck. Death instantaneous on impact."

Cara let out a breath. How could such awful, brutal detail be a relief? But it was. It was. Her worst imaginings weren't true. Hope hadn't suffered, hadn't lain there, trapped, forgotten, to die a slow, awful death.

"Thank you," Gabe said softly.

As usual, St. John let no emotion show. Perhaps the man truly didn't feel any. "Search help," he said bluntly.

"We're calling the sheriff next," Gabe said.

"Undermanned."

"Probably."

"I'll see who's available."

The click of the disconnect echoed in the car's quiet interior.

With a rueful shake of his head, Gabe made the call to the sheriff's office next. He found out in relatively short order that the case had already been transferred from missing persons to homicide, a fact that encouraged Cara even as the words sent a wave of renewed grief through her.

He gave the somewhat harried-sounding investigator what they knew and what they suspected. The man asked enough questions that Cara felt comforted that he wasn't blowing them off. When he disconnected that call, Gabe nodded as if in satisfaction.

"Sounds like he's taking it seriously."

"Yes," Cara agreed.

"Difference between just another missing person and a murder victim."

Cara sucked in a breath. Murder victim. Hope.

"I'm sorry, Cara." Gabe's voice was even grimmer than it had been. She felt his hand on her shoulder, felt the heat of him, took comfort from it. "I was talking in the abstract, I didn't think how it would sound."

"But you're right," Cara said, her voice unsteady. "Hope was murdered."

"Yes," he said.

And in that one syllable Cara heard everything she needed to hear. Gabriel Taggert would never, ever stop until whoever murdered Hope was caught.

They were back on the main road to Pine Lake before she spoke again, more to distract herself from the steep drop-off at the side of the road and memories of what that had meant to Hope than anything else.

"What did St. John mean by search help?"

"I suppose that he'd send Redstone people to help, if necessary."

She shook her head. "I'm beginning to understand what an amazing place that must be to work."

"More than amazing." He glanced at her. "That boat I'm on? Anyone with Redstone has access. Down to the guy who cleans the floors at Redstone Headquarters. Took him out deep-sea fishing last week, with his family, including his little boy who has leukemia."

"Deep-sea fishing? On that gorgeous boat?" Cara asked as she gauged they were a couple of sharp bends out of Pine Lake now.

"Josh's orders. It's what the kid wanted to do."

"That's wonderful," she said, meaning it. "It must be gratifying to—"

"What the hell?" Gabe said sharply.

The crash and the hard jolt came simultaneously. Cara heard a startled gasp, realized it had come from her.

And then she couldn't breathe at all.

They were skidding out of control toward the drop.

Chapter 21

Gabe fought the instinct to hit the brakes just as he fought the wheel of the car. It jerked under his hands as he tried to force it into the skid. His peripheral vision told him they were getting close, too close, to the edge. He wasn't going to have room or time.

Utterly focused, he made a snap decision, the only thing he thought could give them a chance. This was the most solid car he'd ever driven; he was going to have to count on it. The instant he saw road instead of trees through the windshield he hit the accelerator. The powerful motor roared. The rear wheels spun, and for a moment they kept sliding sideways. Then the wheels dug in. For an instant they seemed frozen, motionless.

They shot forward. Not away from the drop. Beside it. Wrong side of the road. Skating perilously close to the edge. But not over it.

He'd gladly settle for that.

When the drive wheels were safely back on asphalt, he steered them back to the right side. There was, thankfully, room on the shoulder, and he pulled off there, with the suddenly comforting mountain beside them rather than the harrowing drop. He applied the brakes carefully, not wanting to hear even a hint of tires spinning on the loose gravel.

Only when they were finally stopped did Gabe look over at Cara. She was pale and wide-eyed, and as he looked he saw her take in a breath and relax a clenched jaw. And then she looked at him.

"Thank you," she said.

He hadn't expected that. "What?"

"For having a cool head and getting us out of that."

He tried to smile, wasn't sure it was more than a grimace. "That wasn't cool. Just instinct. Training."

"Whatever. We're here, and not—" she gestured across the road toward the drop with an eloquent shudder "—down there. No thanks to whoever hit us."

"And contrary to their hopes," he said grimly.

He saw Cara's mouth tighten, knew he didn't have to sugarcoat it, she knew perfectly well this hadn't been an accident.

"Did you see them?" was all she asked. *Talk about cool heads,* he thought in silent salute. "I didn't. I was oblivious, chattering away when I should have been paying attention."

"Paying attention was my job, I was driving," he pointed out. "And I didn't see the truck either, until it was on us."

"Truck?"

"Yes," Gabe said. "A brown pickup. And it was timed perfectly. Just after we rounded that sharp turn. The perfect spot. Steep drop, and not enough straight road behind us to see them coming."

He waited, knowing she'd get there, and quickly. She did. "A brown pickup, like the one at the inn. And someone who knows this road. Well."

"Exactly."

"Crystal," she said.

"My guess," he agreed. "Although I couldn't see the driver. Truck was there so fast all I saw was the front end in the back window."

"And she just kept going."

"She must have been sure she'd taken us out."

"She had reason to be. We couldn't have come much closer."

He saw a faint shiver go through her and knew she was thinking, just as he had, of Hope.

"She must have been so scared, once she knew," Cara whispered.

"It would only have been seconds," Gabe said, reminding her of what St. John had told them.

"An eternity, when you know what's happening."

He couldn't argue with that, so didn't even try.

"But if Crystal was already in town, how did she end up behind us?" Cara asked.

He thought about that for a moment. "Maybe she wasn't in town. Maybe she was along the road somewhere."

"Waiting?" Cara asked, her voice tight. He knew how she felt; lying in wait took it out of the realm of crime of opportunity and into full intent.

"It wouldn't be hard to guess that we'd be leaving Miriam's this morning, now that...we found Hope."

"But if Hope's already been found, why go after us? The sheriff already knows, she couldn't think we hadn't told them."

"But don't forget," Gabe reminded her, "she has no idea we even suspect her."

Cara nodded slowly. "That fight between her and Lawrence. We never did confront her about the cut steering line." She looked out at the road where they'd very nearly replicated Hope's fatal plunge. "Did the truck keep going toward town?"

Gabe's mouth quirked. "I didn't notice. I was a little busy."

She looked back at him quickly. "Saving our lives. I know. It was a rhetorical question, since I was useless in that emergency."

"You didn't shriek," he said. "Believe me, that was useful."

After a moment she lowered her gaze and smiled. A warm smile that sent his blood pulsing through him in hot, heavy beats. And suddenly he wanted this over, so he could focus on what this woman had so quickly come to mean to him. He wanted this over, and her safe, so they could talk. The irony that he wanted the kind of talk men usually ran from in abject terror wasn't lost on him.

But it wasn't over. They were in the middle of it, and it wasn't getting any safer by them just sitting here. It was time to get moving.

He got out to assess the damage. Cara joined him, lending her quick eyes to the task. After a few minutes of inspection, including moving the seriously dented right rear quarter panel—the point of impact—away from the tire with the pry bar from the trunk, he patted the solid coupe on the roof and thanked its makers fervently. He'd have to have it checked, of course, but right now it was drivable.

"Stan?" Cara asked.

"Before we start down, yes," Gabe agreed. "Just to make sure. While he's looking at it, we'll decide what to do."

"And call the sheriff?"

"Yes."

"What if she made a U-turn while we were…spinning, and went back to Miriam's?" Cara asked. "Should I call her?"

"I don't want to tip Crystal off," Gabe said.

"I could make up something."

"But if she finds out you even called, she knows we're not at the bottom of the mountain. And she might run."

Cara nodded in understanding. "But…is Miriam safe?"

Gabe considered that. "I think so. This whole thing seems to be centered on keeping her place with Miriam. So why would she hurt her?"

"That's logical," Cara said. "But is Crystal?"

The truth of what she was saying was undeniable. He'd been thinking as if a woman who had killed once and just now tried again, was rational. Big mistake.

"You're right," he said. "Let's get back to the inn. We'll make calls from there."

She gave him a look he couldn't quite interpret, but said nothing as they got back into the damaged but life-saving car and headed back the way they had come.

* * *

Cara was glad to be sitting down. She felt more shaky after their near miss than she wanted to admit. Oddly, she felt safe enough in the car, with Gabe at the wheel at least. He'd said something about the power and suspension saving them, but she knew it was more his skill and reactions than anything else.

She stole a sideways glance at him. His jaw was set, and he was clearly on hyper alert.

And he'd changed his mind.

She hadn't expected that. She'd been concerned about Miriam, but he'd seemed to have his plan set, and she hadn't thought he would change it to indulge her worries. It was one of the things Hope had always grumbled about. Once he made up his mind, Hope had said, she could rarely get him to change it.

They started out slowly, and she suspected he was testing the car, making sure there wasn't damage that they hadn't found.

"Feels like it's been knocked out of alignment, but other than that, it's amazingly normal," he finally said, picking up speed a little.

"Thank you," she said.

He flicked a glance at her before turning his gaze back to the road and asking, "For what, now?"

"For changing your mind, and going to check on Miriam."

His brows furrowed. "Why wouldn't I? You were right."

"Hope always said..." Her voice trailed away, and she wished she hadn't said it as he glanced at her again and she saw his face.

"Hope," he said carefully, "would change her mind at the drop of a hat. She'd want to back out at the last minute of things planned long ago, where other people were counting on us, simply because she didn't 'feel like it.' Sometimes—" He stopped, as if he were trying to decide whether to say what he was thinking.

"We agreed she wasn't perfect," Cara said, her voice quiet. "And that her being dead, if she was, wouldn't change that. Now that we know it's true, it still doesn't change that."

He didn't comment on what she said, just went on with what he'd started. "Sometimes, she did it just to see what I'd do. To see if I'd give in to her whim, without reason. As if she wanted to see how much control she had over me."

Cara winced, because somewhere in her gut she knew it was true. Hope had played those kinds of games. "She…did that with me, too, sometimes. I never thought about it as a control thing, though. It was just Hope."

They slowed for the turn to Miriam's, and as they sat waiting for an approaching delivery van to pass, he looked at her. "You had a good, solid and logical reason to want to go back to Miriam's. Changing my mind was no problem."

Cara pondered that as they drove toward Miriam's. They once more parked down the road, determined this time that if Crystal was there, they'd catch her alone.

"I don't want Miriam getting in the way or hurt," Gabe said. "If Crystal gets desperate, she might do anything."

Cara nodded, liking his concern for the woman she'd come to care about.

They walked toward the front of the inn, watchful for the bitter young woman. They didn't see her, but spotted the brown truck. They couldn't see any fresh damage from here, but they couldn't see the front end, either. And it was parked, not in its usual spot on the driveway where any new damage would be easily spotted, but up toward the garden shed.

Crystal's territory.

Cara nodded silently as they headed back to the gate they'd gone in before. There was no one in sight this time, so they slipped in and followed the same path they'd taken then.

At the corner of the main building they paused, and Gabe gestured at his ear. Cara's brow furrowed, but then she heard the faint, arrhythmic sound he'd heard.

Clippers. Garden clippers.

Gabe crouched, darted his head around the corner for a quick look, so quick Cara was amazed he'd seen anything.

"She's right there, in the roses," he whispered. "By the first guest cottage."

She kept her voice just as low. "Alone?"

He nodded. "If we split up—" He stopped, looking sorry that he'd said it.

"What?"

He shook his head. "Too dangerous."

"What?" she asked, as insistently as she could in a whisper. When he didn't answer, she looked around. "You mean, while I confront her you go around and come up behind her? In case she tries to run?" He looked startled enough she knew she'd guessed right. "Good idea," she said.

"Rotten idea."

She ignored him. "Go. I'll give you two minutes to get around the other side of the main building. Then I'll go greet her as if nothing were wrong. And we'll see how she reacts."

"Cara—"

"Go," she said. "We'll never have a better chance. I promise, I'll stay more than an arm's length away from her and her clippers. Or rake, if she has it handy."

She wasn't sure what decided him, but something did. He leaned down, planted a quick but luscious kiss on her lips, and then he was gone.

She was so startled—and her response to that kiss so hot and swift—it was a moment before she thought to start tracking that two minutes she'd promised. But when she was sure it had passed, she took a deep breath to steady herself, and began to move.

She went quickly at first, her eyes on Crystal, who was intent on pruning back the rosebush that was nearly waist high and showing spring growth. She was barely ten feet away when Crystal noticed her, and she instantly slowed to a casual stroll, and put a smile on her face. And put out of her mind that she was looking at the woman who had killed her best friend.

"Why, good morning," she said cheerily, all the while watching Crystal's face.

The woman was surprised to see her, there was no doubt

about that. But surprised to see her alive? Cara couldn't tell. And Crystal recovered quickly.

"Thought you were gone," she snarled.

"I'm sure you did," Cara said. "How was your trip to town?"

The young woman looked puzzled. "Useless. Didn't have what I needed."

The expression looked genuine, Cara thought.

Crystal went on bluntly, as if to say they weren't welcome any longer, "Miriam didn't expect you back. Had me strip the rooms." She gave Cara a look she couldn't quite interpret. "Not that you used both of them last night."

Cara felt color rise in her cheeks, the last thing she wanted when face-to-face with this woman. Especially since she'd just seen Gabe, just beyond the arbor a few feet behind Crystal.

"Don't blame you," Crystal said. "He's a hot one."

Cara blinked. And Crystal smiled. A real, sincere smile, and it changed the hard, set lines of her face. For that moment, she looked her age, instead of eons older. And for that moment, Cara had no idea what to say.

But the smile vanished quickly, and Crystal's face settled back into her usual sullen expression as she tossed her thick braid over her shoulder and went back to her pruning. With those clippers.

"Yes, he is," Cara finally managed, carefully avoiding another glance at Gabe. "I feel guilty, though. Hope was my best friend."

"She's dead, I hear. Sorry."

Cara took a deep breath. "Are you?"

Crystal gave her a sideways look. "Not really. All flash. Didn't like her."

Cara caught Gabe's movement. She wondered if he was closing in because of what Crystal had said, or because she was getting close to why they were here.

"So you wanted her to go."

"Wasn't sorry."

"Because she shared something with Miriam you never could."

Crystal shrugged, as if indifferent. "They were tight."

"And you felt threatened."

Crystal looked at her then. "By her? She'd no more do what I do around here than fly."

"But she took up Miriam's time, and attention. Weren't you worried she wouldn't have any left to give you?"

Crystal laughed. It wasn't a pleasant sound, and the suspicions that had wavered slightly came flooding back full force.

"You think I was looking for a mother figure or something? Hell with that. They're overrated. I get food and a roof here. Miriam doesn't give it. I earn it."

This was getting her nowhere. Crystal was back at the roses, so Cara glanced over at Gabe. He nodded, and she knew he meant she should just cut to the chase.

"So why would you risk that? We were leaving anyway. Why try to kill us?"

Crystal's clipping stopped. She turned her head to look at Cara. Better than lunging at me, Cara thought. Not that she'd have gotten away with it; Gabe was moving now.

"What the hell are you talking about?"

"You trying to kill us like you did Hope," she said, with a bluntness that more than equaled Crystal's usual tone.

Crystal backed up a step. Then another.

"Going somewhere?" Gabe asked pleasantly.

Crystal yelped, jerked, turned as if she were going to run. But Gabe was right there, blocking her retreat.

"It's over, Linda," Gabe said, and Cara saw the woman pale as he said her real name.

"You're crazy," she said. "Both of you. I never killed anyone."

"You sent Hope driving down the mountain to her death," Cara said.

"But you and your truck didn't succeed with us this morning," Gabe said. "You should have stuck around to be sure we went over the edge."

Crystal frowned then. "Truck? I haven't driven that truck in a month."

"Nice try. You already admitted you went into town."

"I walked." She looked from Cara to Gabe and back again. "I don't have a driver's license."

"So law-abiding citizen that you are, you don't drive? Please," Cara said.

"It's over," Gabe said again. "You got away with killing my wife for eight years. You tried to kill us, twice, because we got too close."

Crystal burst into motion. She bent, grabbed a pruning saw Cara hadn't seen from the ground beside her, and in the same movement lunged at Cara.

The glint of the nasty blade left little doubt in Cara's mind.

Crystal would kill again if she had to.

Chapter 22

Gabe's heart slammed as he saw Crystal grab the wicked little saw and lunge toward Cara. Adrenaline poured through him as Cara darted to one side, putting the rose bush and its thorns between her and her attacker, and giving him the split second he needed.

He tackled Crystal. They went down in a pile of bark mulch. Rolled. Gabe tried to dodge the nasty blade. Crystal tried to hack off whatever she could reach to escape. Gabe felt a sharp rush of pain as the blade connected with his left shoulder. He tried again to pin Crystal, this time taking no care; female or not, she was dangerous, and had to be stopped.

Crystal suddenly yelped in pain of her own. She recoiled, giving him the leverage he needed. In the next second he had her face down, pinned with his knee. And over them both stood Cara, Crystal's rake in her hands, ready to jab again if necessary.

"Nice work," Gabe said.

Cara didn't smile. "You're bleeding," she said anxiously.

He tested his arm, his hand. It hurt, but everything worked. "It'll keep for the moment."

"Hey!"

The shout came from behind them, and they both looked that way in time to see Lawrence Hammon trotting toward them, a look of shock on his face.

"What's going on? What happened?" He paled slightly at the sight of Gabe's bloodied arm. "My God, she's finally done it, hasn't she? I knew it."

His gaze was fastened on Crystal, who was busy trying to spit out pieces of decorative bark.

"You knew what, Lawrence?" Cara asked as Gabe got Crystal to her feet, keeping her under control with an arm twisted behind her back.

"I knew she was crazy. Dangerous."

"Dangerous?" Gabe asked.

Lawrence looked at him. "I didn't know who you were related to, when we met before. But I was here, the last time your wife was here."

Gabe went still. Crystal twisted, her eyes fastened on Lawrence now as she spat out, "Yes, you were, you son of a bitch."

Lawrence ignored her. "I'm sorry about her, by the way. She seemed nice, the few times I met her." The banal nicety sounded oddly out of place in the current circumstances. But Lawrence soldiered on. "Now it all makes sense. I caught her—" he gestured toward Crystal "—messing around with your wife's car, that last time."

"You're a damned liar!"

Lawrence ignored Crystal's shout. "I thought she was just trying to steal something. That's what she usually does. But she had those clippers, like she always has."

Crystal let out a string of epithets that would do the saltiest sailor proud.

"Now I realize what she was really doing." He shook his head mournfully. "I've tried over and over to get Mom to do the sensible thing, and get rid of her. But that soft heart of hers...."

"Damn you!" Crystal shouted. She twisted in Gabe's grasp. He tightened his grip, ignoring the jab of pain from the slice on his shoulder; the bleeding had mostly stopped, so he knew it wasn't serious.

"I'll call the sheriff," Cara said, taking her cell phone out of her pocket. At least she'd thought to do that, Gabe thought. His was stupidly still in the car.

"You're believing him, aren't you?" Crystal said. Rage reddened her face. "He's lying through his teeth and you believe him."

Cara flipped open the phone, but looked at Crystal before dialing. "Lying about what?" she asked.

"Everything!" Crystal seemed to make an effort to steady herself. "Look, I know what you think of me, what everyone around here thinks of me. But Miriam's been good to me, one of the only people who ever has been, and I wouldn't do anything to someone she cared about. Unlike *him*," she finished with a vehemence aimed at Lawrence that startled Gabe.

Lawrence backed up a step, looking at Crystal much like Gabe would imagine he'd look at a coiled rattlesnake.

"Nice try," Gabe said. "But what reason would he have to hurt my wife?"

"And a friend of his own mother?" Cara added.

"Exactly," Lawrence said.

"I'll tell you," Crystal said. "In one word. Lorna."

Gabe blinked. But before he could ask Crystal what she meant, Lawrence took a step toward them. Gabe felt Crystal tense, as if she expected a physical attack. He wondered if he was going to end up in the strange position of protecting the woman who'd murdered his wife.

"Don't you dare! You're not fit to even speak my sister's name."

"There!" Crystal said. "You see what I mean?"

Gabe frowned. So did Cara, as she said, "No. What do you mean?"

"Don't you see? He's crazy! He's obsessed, he's never let go of his dead sister."

"That's ridiculous," Lawrence said. "Are you calling the sheriff, or shall I? I want her gone from here."

Crystal glared at him. "You think I'm blind? That I didn't see or hear your fights with Miriam?"

She looked at Cara, apparently thinking she was her best chance. A torrent of words poured out, more than they'd ever heard from her before.

"He was convinced Hope was trying to become a replacement for his dead sister. That she was taking Lorna's place, in Miriam's heart. They were getting too close. You were right about that, they shared something Miriam and I never would. That didn't matter to me, she was already giving more than I'd ever had in my life. But he—" Gabe still had her arms pinned, so she kicked toward Lawrence "—was the one who was threatened by that. So he decided he had to get rid of her."

"Can't you shut her up?" Lawrence said to Gabe. "This is absurd, having to listen to this."

"I'm the one who caught *him* messing with Hope's car," Crystal said. "Right before she left that last time." She looked at Lawrence again. "*He's* the one who was driving the truck this morning. I saw him get out of it when he came back."

"That's preposterous," Lawrence exclaimed.

"Ask Miriam. She knows I've been out here working all morning," Crystal said, looking from Cara to Gabe and back, a pleading in her eyes Gabe would have never expected to see there. And he remembered that moment in the kitchen, when Crystal had seemed protective of Miriam.

"Gabe," Cara said softly. "The story. The last one she wrote, before that last trip here…."

Gabe's brows furrowed. He'd automatically looked at the dates on all the writings Hope had sent Miriam, remembered the one that had been sent right before she'd come up that last time. The one that had puzzled them, because in it Hope had made no mention of an immediate visit, had only said she'd see Miriam next month, as planned.

And then it hit him. That was the story where she'd mentioned Lawrence. That he'd driven into Pine Lake behind her as she headed home.

The story where she'd jokingly mentioned that you could surely tell Lawrence lived down on the flat, because he drove like a city maniac, tailgating all the way, not easygoing and courteous like all the mountain residents were. He was the exception to the village friendliness, she'd written, the only truly unwelcoming soul she'd found here. And then she had, Hope-like, forgiven him, because he was such a lost soul, still grieving fiercely for his long dead sister.

Tailgating.

Unwelcoming.

Grieving.

Cara's words came back to him in a rush. "Grief does crazy things to you," he said softly.

"Yes," Cara said.

"What are you wasting time for?" Lawrence demanded.

They both turned to look at him.

"Call the sheriff," he said. "Or I will. Don't you want her to pay for what she did?"

"Did you try to run Hope off the road the way you did us, first?" Gabe asked; he wasn't sure he believed it, but he watched Lawrence's face as he went on. "And when that didn't work, you cut her brake line?"

Lawrence paled. And backed up a step. "Don't be stupid."

"And was Crystal just handy?" Cara asked. "A likely scape-goat that no one would believe anyway?"

Lawrence switched his gaze to Cara. "You can't be taking her seriously! Look at her. She's nothing, a stray, a step away from jail all her life."

"Is that why you didn't try to kill her?" Gabe asked. "She was no threat, not like Hope, who shared a talent and a love of writing with your mother?"

"He did try."

Gabe looked at Crystal. He still had a firm grip on her, but she'd quit fighting the moment they'd started to listen to her. He'd noticed, and it had been part of the reason he'd turned the probing questions on Lawrence.

"First he tried to buy me off. Offered me money to leave. Then he tried to drive me away. General nastiness, pranks, then he really got ugly. Tried to poison me, with stuff from his own mother's garden shed."

"That's a lie!" But Lawrence was backing up quickly now, his eyes darting around nervously.

"What would your sainted sister think of you now, Larry?" Crystal sneered.

"She'd understand," Lawrence spat back at her. "She always did. She was the only one who ever did."

Gabe was expecting it when Lawrence broke and ran. He'd already made his decision, and he let go of Crystal and went after Lawrence. Cara reacted almost as quickly, grabbing up Crystal's dropped pruning saw and darting toward him, making him reverse course. It was just the split second Gabe needed and he took the man down with a knee-popping tackle.

They scuffled, Lawrence flailing wildly. He landed a lucky hit on Gabe's cheekbone but then suddenly stopped, curling up like one of the sow bugs that populated the garden debris, screaming, "Stop, stop!"

Gabe rolled off the man. He looked at the new assailant; Crystal had finally gotten to put her rake to use. He let her get in a couple of good licks before he gently stopped her.

"Enough, Crystal. He'll get his, now."

She delivered one more blow to the quivering Lawrence, but then she backed up and dropped the rake.

Cara reached out and put a hand on Crystal's arm. Somewhat to Gabe's surprise, the woman didn't shake it off.

"Now I really will call the sheriff," Cara said.

"You believed me," Crystal said, sounding astonished.

"Yes," Gabe said.

Crystal looked from Cara to Gabe. And for the first time since they'd known her she looked, not angry, but genuinely troubled. "I'm sorry," she said. "I was sure he'd done it, but I had no way to prove it. And I knew no one would believe me."

Gabe imagined apologizing was not something Crystal did often. "I understand," he said.

Cara paused in the act of dialing the phone. "Why did you stay, after he tried to poison you?"

"Miriam," Crystal said simply. "I couldn't be sure he wouldn't get even crazier and decide she deserved to die for trying to replace his precious sister."

This time it was Gabe who reached out and put a hand on her arm. "Crazy indeed. You can't replace someone you loved."

Cara made a sound, then finished dialing the call to the sheriff.

"I've never loved anybody like that," Crystal said, "but that doesn't mean I don't know how it works." She glanced at Gabe's bloody shoulder. "I'm sorry about that, too."

At the second apology in as many minutes, Gabe smiled. "It's all right." He glanced at Lawrence, still curled up in a fetal position on the ground. "He's lucky he didn't have the guts to take you on face-to-face. You would have taken him out in a minute."

She gave him the first real smile he'd ever seen on the young woman's face. And for an instant he saw what she might have been, had her life gone differently. A sudden idea occurred to him, and he made a mental note of it.

"It just never occurred to me," Cara said softly.

"What?" Gabe asked.

"That he meant Hope, too, when he talked of his mother taking in strays."

Gabe winced inwardly. "Me, neither. If it had, I might have thought of him sooner. But this explains why he reacted that way when we broke up that fight between him and Crystal. I thought he was hesitating to talk about something personal, when in fact he was trying to think up that lie about the antique watches."

Things happened quickly after that; a single sheriff's deputy, a young man who looked barely out of the academy, arrived to assess the situation and quickly call for backup and a supervisor when Gabe informed him he needed to take custody of a murderer. While he handcuffed Lawrence Hammon, Crystal went inside to find Miriam, insisting on telling her herself. Miriam was writing again, behind closed doors, and could tune out the world, Crystal told them.

"If she's going to hate me for ratting him out, then I want to know now," she said.

"Gently, Crystal," Cara said. "He's her son."

"And a pitiful excuse for one."

"Perhaps. But still…."

"I'll be gentle." She glanced at both of them. "I can be, if I want to."

"I think," Gabe said quietly, "you can be a lot of good things, if you want to be."

That startled her. So much that twice on her way into the house, she turned and looked back. And when Gabe glanced back to Cara, she was smiling so warmly it took his breath away.

Cara and Gabe followed as the deputy put Lawrence into the back of the black-and-white car parked in front of the inn. There was no sign yet of Miriam, and for that Cara was thankful. There was no way this couldn't be awful for the kind, generous woman, and Cara regretted that. But they'd had to do it. For Hope.

While the deputy was in the middle of taking their statements, still waiting for his sergeant to arrive, a big four-wheel-drive crew cab pickup with the name "Callahan Aviation Services" written on the side pulled up in front of the inn. Two men got out and walked toward them. Neither was the man who'd met them when they'd gone to the airport, George Callahan. Not that she could figure out why he'd be here anymore than these two strangers. Although one of them did look vaguely familiar, she thought.

Both were tall, one about Gabe's height with close-clipped dark hair, the other, the one that seemed familiar, even taller, with longer dark hair faintly touched with silver at the temples. The first man strode toward them in a way that reminded her of Gabe. The taller, lanky man seemed to simply stroll as if they had all the time in the world and yet, she noticed, had no trouble staying even.

"Holy—" Gabe bit back however he'd been going to finish the exclamation. "Talk about sending out the cavalry."

"What?" Cara asked.

"I don't know who the other guy is," he muttered, "but you're about to get your wish to meet Josh Redstone."

Cara smothered a gasp. That was why he'd looked familiar; she'd seen his picture several times in various business publications. The articles had always emphasized his unassuming demeanor, his casual approach, but the photographs had always seemed stiff and formal. Now, in reality, he looked like nothing more than what some detractors—jealous rivals, she'd always thought—called him, a cowboy with freakish luck.

As if you could build an empire like Redstone on just luck, she'd thought then.

And now, as the two men stopped before them and Joshua Redstone turned a pair of steady gray eyes on her, she knew she'd been right. When he spoke, she also understood why those detractors had fallen prey to their own misconceptions.

"Gabe," Josh said, holding out a hand, taking Gabe's in a firm shake. He raised his other hand as if to clap Gabe on the other shoulder, noticed the blood and pulled his hand back. His expression quickly morphed into a frown. "What's this? St. John didn't say anything about you being hurt."

"He didn't know. It's fine. I'll get it cleaned up and be good to go."

Josh seemed to assess that for a moment, then accepted it. He gestured at the man who'd come with him.

"Gabe Taggert, Noah Rider."

Cara saw Gabe's eyes widen. "Rider? Redstone's premier point man? What are you doing here?"

The man grinned as Cara tried to figure out why just as Josh's face had seemed familiar, this man's name did. "I happened to have the good fortune of being in Josh's office when he got word you might need some help up here. I sort of invited myself along to escape the boredom."

"And Paige will have my hide when she finds out I let you hitch a ride into what turned out to be a murder case," Josh said, his mouth twisting wryly.

Rider laughed. "Don't forget my wife and I met during a terrorist hostage-taking."

Cara felt the urge to gasp again, but quashed it. She'd read about that incident at the Redstone Resort in the papers, where guerrilla rebels from a neighboring Caribbean island had taken a school full of children hostage. And this was the man who'd saved them, all of them.

And, she realized belatedly, he was probably the point man Gabe had mentioned before, the one Tess had flown out of the Colombian jungle under fire.

"You must be Cara," Josh said, jerking her attention back. He held out his hand, and as she took it, Cara thought what a crazy turn her life had taken in the past three days, to end up standing here shaking hands with multi-billionaire Josh Redstone. "I'm Josh Redstone. This is Noah Rider who, no matter what he says, could never be bored, not married to Paige and with twins on the way."

"Congratulations," Cara said, looking at Rider. Then, to Josh, "I…can't believe you came yourself."

He shrugged, as if it were nothing. "Gabe needed help. I was the one not doing anything important at the moment."

"And the one who could fly," Rider put in.

Josh grinned. "There is that. And I had just been into that airport not so long ago."

"I hope you were gentler with Reeve than you were with me," Rider said, but the smile on his face belied the complaint. "But it seems we're too late to help much."

"You can save us from spending hours giving statements of the same thing over and over again," Gabe suggested.

"Now that," Rider said, "I can do."

And in that moment, what she saw in the man's eyes made her very confident that somehow, the law enforcement maze would be threaded more easily.

Josh's expression turned serious then. "Can I talk to you for a minute, Gabe? Privately?"

They walked away a few feet, and Cara saw Josh put a hand on Gabe's arm as he listened intently. After a few words Gabe went very still, paled slightly, and Cara's stomach knotted. She didn't know what Josh had told him, wasn't sure she wanted to know. Perhaps it wasn't anything to do with this, perhaps it was something work-related, some bad news there. Because what on earth could be worse than knowing Hope had been murdered?

She found out a short while later, when Josh and Noah Rider had gone off to smooth a path for them and they were about to go inside to face, reluctantly, the woman whose son they'd just had arrested.

But on the wide front porch of the cheerful yellow inn, Gabe stopped. Cara looked up at him. Then, bluntly, in a flat voice unlike any she'd heard from him, he told her what Josh had told him.

"St. John pulled some more of his strings."

"And?" She held her breath, waiting.

"Hope was pregnant."

Before Cara could even absorb this shock, a gasp from the doorway turned them both around. Miriam stood there, staring at them.

"Oh, my God. It's my fault," she said.

Chapter 23

"It's my fault. It's all my fault."

"Stop that, Miriam. It's not your fault."

Gabe and Cara stood in the kitchen, watching Crystal try to comfort her benefactor.

"She's right," Cara said gently. "Lawrence made his decisions, he's a grown-up. You had nothing to do with it."

"I didn't mean Lawrence," Miriam said, startling them all. "I...can't deal with that, not yet. I meant Hope."

Cara glanced at Gabe, saw by his furrowed brows that he had no more idea what Miriam meant than she did.

"How was what happened to Hope your fault?" Cara asked gently.

"You said she was pregnant."

Cara didn't dare look at Gabe again, she didn't want to see what might be in his face, his eyes. His beloved Hope had been carrying his child, a child he'd obviously never known about, a child who had died with her.

The second miracle, Cara thought with an ache in her chest.

"What does that have to do with what happened?" Gabe asked. His voice was level, even, and only the tightness of the muscles along his jaw told Cara what an effort it was.

"I made her promise me that if it ever happened, I'd be the second to know. After you."

Gabe let out a compressed breath. "And I was deployed," he muttered. "It could have been days before we could talk."

Miriam rubbed at her reddened eyes as tears brimmed once more. "Why didn't she just call me?"

"She would have wanted to share it in person," Cara said of the friend she'd known so well.

"I shouldn't have made her make that promise. But I told her that, after losing Lorna, this would be as close as I'd ever come to having a daughter to share that with. She promised. And died trying to keep that promise."

Miriam broke down then. Crystal never left her side, and urged her gently into the other room to lie down.

"She must feel destroyed. First her son, now this," Cara said.

Gabe said nothing, and finally Cara looked at him. He said in that same, flat voice, "Redstone will help, if we can. Anything she needs."

"I hope that's short of a slick lawyer for Lawrence," Cara said.

Gabe said nothing, didn't even react.

"I'm sorry, Gabe," she said. "I can't even begin to imagine how you must feel. First Hope, then...a child you never even knew about? I'm so sorry."

When he still said nothing, Cara reached out and touched his uninjured arm. It was rock-solid beneath her fingers. And still he didn't react.

"Gabe?"

He wouldn't even look at her. Cara's heart sank. Somehow in the past few minutes, everything had changed between them.

What did you expect? He just found out he would have been—

should have been—a father. A child with Hope, the woman he had loved. And probably still loves.

Gabe's words to Miriam came back to her, painfully.

You can't replace someone you loved.

She didn't have the heart or the time to press further. Josh and Rider descended on them, having organized things in an almost frighteningly efficient manner. The statements they'd already given would stand for now; the sheriff's office would contact them later for more. Gabe's car would be towed down for repairs, Rider told them, while the two of them flew back with him and Josh in the jet Josh had flown here. The *Hawk III*, he said, the only one that could handle the limitations of the high-altitude airport's runway length.

"Do you want me to call Hope's folks?" Josh asked Gabe as they drove in the big pickup back to the airport, Cara and Gabe in the backseat of the cab.

"No."

Cara had known that would be his answer. He would never let someone else do a job he felt was his responsibility.

Josh nodded in understanding, as if he'd never expected anything else. The fact that he'd made the offer anyway told Cara that the stories—legends, really—about this man were apparently true; if you worked for him, you were family.

"We'll get you back home," Rider said as they pulled in once more at Callahan Aviation. There on the apron, where before the Redstone chopper had sat, was a sleek little private jet in the same colors. "And once we're there, if I can help, you just say so. Anything you need, Gabe, to make arrangements, you've got it."

Rider and Josh got out of the truck, leaving them alone for the moment. And Cara belatedly realized Rider had meant arrangements for some kind of funeral for Hope. And for the first time the utter finality of what she'd always suspected but apparently never completely accepted hit her. Tears welled up suddenly. She fought not to break down sobbing, but it was a useless effort. She felt the urge to lean into Gabe, to seek comfort with the man who had given her such joy, but he'd made it clear he wanted nothing to do with her right now.

Maybe ever, she thought. *Maybe it was just too much to overcome, Hope, this news, all of it.*

So instead she leaned against the door of the truck, trying to keep the weeping she was helpless to stop as quiet as she could.

And then Gabe was there; he'd moved closer, awkwardly put his arm around her. Pulled her close where she'd wanted to be, leaning against him, taking strength and warmth from him. For a long time they just sat there, Cara weeping, Gabe holding her, until she couldn't stop herself from looking up at him through the tears, wondering what he was feeling.

The moment they made eye contact, he drew in a deep breath.

"What Hope went through," he began, then stopped as if it were beyond words.

"Yes," Cara said, steadying herself with an effort; if Gabe was ready to talk, she had to be ready to listen. He deserved that. "But now we know. Why she was here, and what the second miracle was."

"Yes," Gabe said. Then, after a moment, he went on. "I can't picture the guy I was then as a father. Not a good one, anyway. I was too young, too focused on my career."

"But maybe Hope would have been…happier."

"Maybe."

They sat in silence. Once, Cara looked out to see Josh talking with George Callahan, whose crew was readying the red and gray little jet for flight.

"I still can't believe Josh Redstone himself just hopped in one of his planes and flew up here to help."

"That's Josh," Gabe said. "Rider surprised me more."

"So, is everybody who works for Redstone like you two, and Tess and Ryan? So loyal and dedicated?"

"Pretty much," Gabe said. "He inspires it."

Cara thought later, after they'd landed and taxied over to the Redstone hangar, that she wished she had been in a better frame of mind to enjoy this. The *Hawk III* was something: sleek, quick, and elegant. And Josh Redstone was obviously a pilot who knew what he was doing; she'd never had such a whisper-soft landing.

The rest was a blur; Josh himself cleaned up Gabe's shoulder, and offered him a clean shirt from a locker inside the hangar. Rider drove them back to the marina, where it had all started what seemed like ages ago, and where Cara's car was parked. Through it all, Gabe and Cara never spoke, at least, not to each other.

The boat Gabe commanded now sat docilely at the dock, yet still looked as if it could fly in its own way as gracefully as the *Hawk III*. Cara wondered idly if there was any end to the designs the fertile mind of Josh Redstone could come up with.

Gabe gave Rider a quick tour of the boat, then the Redstone point man left with a promise to be in touch to see what was needed.

And then it was only the two of them, standing in the boat's salon in almost exactly the spot where they'd first seen each other again. For a long moment silence spun out between them.

"Cara—"

"Gabe—"

They both stopped, looking rueful.

"Awkward," Gabe muttered.

"Yes."

He reached out then, put his hands on her shoulders. "I'm not that kid I was with Hope anymore. If I met the both of you for the first time now, I'm not sure it would be her I'd be looking at."

Cara's breath caught.

"I want to see you again, Cara. I want you in my life. I want more days, and—" his voice went husky "—nights."

She hadn't thought, hadn't dared to think of this as a possibility. Those words, coming from this man, were a dream come true. But it was a dream she'd never had the right to dream. And even now that she knew Hope was truly gone, she wasn't sure she could bring herself to take what had once been hers. And he was in turmoil, coping with confirmation of their worst fears, and the shocking knowledge that Hope had been pregnant. The loss had to be astounding, and she suspected that was behind his words.

"I...not now, Gabe. It's not the time." She could hardly believe she was saying it, turning away what she'd once longed for so much. But she couldn't do anything else. "I won't be a consolation prize, Gabe. And I could never replace Hope. I won't even try."

He released her abruptly, took a step back. For a moment he said nothing, then, slowly, "I understand."

And that was it. The last words between them, except a forced casual goodbye as she got into the car she'd parked there—had it really only been three days ago?—and drove away. She forced herself not to look in the rearview mirror at him. What had brought them together again, their love for Hope, now lay as an impassable roadblock between them.

Chapter 24

"What's going on, Cap?"

Gabe turned to look at his first mate. "No idea. Josh said head to these coordinates and wait, so that's what we're doing."

It had taken him a while in the beginning, to get used to explaining things like that. In the navy, a captain didn't usually explain a simple order. But then, in the navy, the first mate likely would never have asked. But now he did it without much thought; this was a different world, and in the end, he valued it just as much, if not more.

"Weird," Mark said, but in a tone that was more conversational than judgmental. "Just sitting here, a couple hundred miles out. But if it's what the man wants…."

"Exactly."

Mark grinned. "Not like anybody's gonna argue with him, even if they wanted to, which nobody does."

"Exactly," Gabe repeated, managing a brief smile back.

It was all he could manage. He hadn't been in a smiling mood for five weeks now. Ever since the day Cara had gotten in her car and driven out of his life as abruptly as she'd dropped back into it. He'd only seen her once since, at Lawrence Hammon's court appearance. They'd barely acknowledged each other.

"Sir?"

He refocused on Mark, realizing he'd lost it again, standing here on the bow staring out at blue water unseeingly, he who once would have seen every swell, every ripple that indicated current, every wind wave that told him how to adjust the boat to maintain the position they'd been sitting in for several hours now.

"About your wife. I'm really sorry."

Mark's tone held genuine sympathy, but also trepidation, as if it had taken him this five weeks to work up the nerve to speak about it. That was what made Gabe force himself to respond.

"Thank you." He sounded a bit sharp even to himself, so he added, "It's been a long time. It's not…raw. But thank you."

Mark nodded, and lowered his gaze as if afraid he'd offended his boss. Gabe took pity on him and said in a near-normal voice, "Check for any new weather advisories, will you? I want to be sure that front isn't coming any farther south."

"Yes, sir." Mark turned smartly on his heel and left.

He'd driven the crew hard in the last five weeks. The first two were spent pushing the boat to its limits, and true to most Redstone designs, she'd held steady and firm, requiring only small adjustments here and there as things settled in. The last three had been spent fine-tuning the crew in much the same way; for all the relaxed atmosphere, Redstone vessels were run at utmost efficiency. The ease aboard ship didn't come easily.

He'd driven himself even harder, overseeing everything personally, until he was fairly sure most of the crew wished he would back off. But they'd never say anything, not when they all thought he was grieving for his murdered wife.

Too bad he himself wasn't convinced of it. But it was hard to sell the idea that he was grieving for Hope when all he could think about was Cara.

I won't be a consolation prize, Gabe.

Had he given her the idea that he was trying to replace Hope? he wondered. That he'd wanted her because she'd been Hope's best friend? Had he made her feel that her connection to his dead wife was the only reason he wanted her?

Was it the truth?

He'd been wrestling with that for five weeks now, and was no closer to an answer. Countless times he'd wanted to call her, just to hear her voice, but his doubts had stopped him. Above all the doubt that she would want to talk to him, if that was how he'd made her feel.

"Sir?" Mark was back.

Gabe gave himself an inward shake. "What is it, Mark?"

"You've got a call on the bridge. Mr. Redstone."

Gabe nodded and started back toward the outside stairs. "Maybe now we'll find out why we're here."

A few minutes later, he had a partial answer, and sent Mark to round up the helipad crew to get it ready for an incoming flight.

"You've got about an hour," Josh said.

"All right."

"How are you, Gabe?"

"Fine." He almost, instinctively, added a "sir" but held it back. "We'll be ready," he said instead.

"Good. And don't worry about Cara. If she needs anything, we'll see she gets it."

Gabe went still. "Cara?"

"I'm sure she'll be fine. But if she needs special care, Redstone will—"

"What's wrong?" Gabe cut off his boss without a thought as his heart began to hammer in his chest.

"You haven't talked to her?"

"Not since Hammon's arraignment. What's wrong?"

"I don't have all the details. Just that she's not doing well."

Gabe felt a queasiness in his stomach as a sweat broke out on his body. "Josh, I—"

"I've got to go, Gabe. I'll see if I can find out more and let you know."

With that Josh hung up as abruptly as his right-hand man, St. John. Gabe just stood there, his hand clenched around the handheld microphone that accessed the Redstone satellite com system.

He sat down abruptly in the captain's chair. *Cara.* What was wrong? Hideous possibilities raced through his mind in rapid succession.

"Sir?" Mark's voice held genuine concern this time. "Are you all right?"

No, he thought as his heart hammered as if it were trying to beat its way out of his chest.

Definitely not, he added, suddenly aware he wasn't breathing so much as gasping for air.

He couldn't just sit here and wait to find out. If he wasn't bound by Josh's orders to stay put, he'd already have this boat headed to port.

He was thinking about it anyway.

He told Mark he was fine and to give him a minute, then belatedly grabbed his cell phone. It wouldn't work out here, but it had Cara's number. He got it, then picked up the more private, receiver version of the satellite phone and dialed.

It immediately went to voice mail, telling him the phone was turned off. He shivered at the sound of her voice on the recording, wondering how he'd gone so long without hearing it. He left a message he was sure was disjointed and confused, but he hadn't thought beyond calling to what he'd say.

She's all right. She has to be. I can't lose her, too.

It hit him then, that somehow, on some level, his mind, or his gut—or his heart—had been working on this. And now the answer was perfectly clear; Cara Thorpe was no replacement for Hope. And she was certainly no consolation prize. She was the woman he'd been waiting for, and looking for. The one with the solid, steady center Hope had lacked, the one with the resources to handle whatever life threw at her with style and grace.

He began to pace the bridge, barely managing to resist calling Josh back and telling him he couldn't wait here, he had to get to Cara. And then it occurred to him that he could hitch a ride back in the Redstone chopper and get to shore a lot quicker than by riding this boat back. Whatever this VIP guest needed could be handled by the crew he'd drilled so relentlessly the last three weeks. And if Josh didn't like the desertion of his captain, well….

Over the next half hour he tried Cara's cell every few minutes. Then he gave up and went to stand on the stern deck near the raised helipad, trusting Mark to hold the boat steady into the wind for the landing. He put on the headset that would allow him to talk to the incoming pilot. The two-person crew responsible for keeping the helipad safe and bringing in aircraft kept giving him curious looks, but he said nothing. All the patience he'd ever learned seemed to have vanished.

"Incoming!"

The voice came over the PA, and he and the two crew members scanned the horizon. Patty spotted it first, and yelped the sighting. Gabe followed her gesture and spotted the helicopter heading toward them.

It was the same chopper that had flown them through the mountains, Gabe thought with a qualm. And judging by the way the pilot negotiated the headwind, bringing the craft to a hover just in front of the pad, then backing down to a whisper-soft landing even on a pitching target, Tess Machado was likely at the controls.

"Nice landing," he said into the headset.

Tess's voice came back at him. "It's like rotor-heads tell the starch-wings who think they're better pilots— 'Yeah, but how fast can you fly backwards?'"

He could see her grin through the bubble, and managed a smile; something about Tess's grin was infectious even through his worry. And today there was something even more delightful about her usual cheerful expression.

The rotors began to slow as she disengaged. She left the engine running as she got out, telling Gabe she was planning a quick departure. He wondered if he should tell her now that she was going to have a passenger on the return trip.

"Got a present for you," she called, and opened the passenger compartment door, where someone was just getting free of the harness. A woman, who slid out of the helicopter in an obvious hurry.

Cara.

He gaped up at her. She spotted him and froze, staring back.

He stood stock-still, unable to believe she was there at all, let alone apparently perfectly healthy. The breeze from the slowing rotors was still enough to stir her hair, and it glinted bright copper in the sun. She had one hand to her mouth as she stared at him in obvious surprise.

"Cara," he said.

She couldn't hear him over the chopper's engine. Finally galvanized he started up the steps just as she started down. They met on the third step and he grabbed her, letting out a heartfelt oath at the feel of her in his arms again. He swung her down to the deck and leaped down beside her.

"I thought you were sick!"

"Josh told me you were hurt!"

"I'm fine."

"So am I."

"No, you're not," Tess said from above. "You're two stubborn, wary people and you're letting history get in your way. Anybody who's seen you together knows you belong that way."

They gaped at her in unison; they had obviously been had, in a big, Redstone-style way.

"You're clear to head in, now, Gabe," Tess said with a grin. "We figure it'll take you about eight hours to get to port since Josh forbids you to run at top speed. Enough time even for you two to work things out."

Before they could even react to that, Tess was back aboard the chopper. The rotors picked up speed, their pitch changed, and in moments she was lifting off as smoothly as she'd landed.

In the silence Tess's departure left behind, Gabe was vaguely aware the deck had suddenly become deserted. There was no crew in sight, and he wondered if Tess or Josh had manipulated that, too.

Not that it mattered. The only thing that really mattered was that Cara was all right, and here in his arms.

"I was about to get on that bird," he said against her hair. "I didn't care about my job, this boat, anything except getting to you."

"I did get on that silly bird," Cara said, "even though I swore I never would again. I was afraid otherwise I might not get here in time."

"We," Gabe said wryly, "have been had."

"Yes."

He looked down at her. "But with the best of intentions."

"Yes," she repeated.

He hesitated for a moment, then decided to hell with it, he'd waited long enough.

"You were wrong, Cara. I never, ever thought of you as a replacement for Hope. How could I, when you fill places in me she never did?"

He heard her draw in a sharp breath, saw her eyes widen, and knew he'd somehow found the right words.

"And you could never be any man's idea of a consolation prize. *You're the* prize, Cara. And I'll do whatever it takes to win."

"Too late," she said.

Gabe's breath died in his throat. Had he left it too long? Then she smiled at him, and he could take in air again.

"That contest," she said, "is already over."

He pulled her tighter and took her mouth with a ferocity that had five weeks of longing and aching for her behind it. And when, later, he introduced her to the captain's quarters and they locked the door, he barely noticed that there still wasn't a crew member in sight.

Epilogue

Cara looked down at the small, richly bound book in her hands. The gold lettering embossed on the cover and spine gleamed in the California sun, catching the light. Another glint caught her eye, and she smiled as she looked at the diamond on her left hand. This was the last day her engagement ring would be on her finger by itself.

As she watched Gabe drive the expertly repaired Lexus, she thought about the last time they'd made this trip. It had been the last of three destinations, the one they'd feared the most.

The first, a quick flight to Oregon—thankfully too far for the chopper, meaning she got to enjoy this trip on the bigger *Hawk IV*—netted them the surprised but pleased approval of her parents, especially her father, who appreciated Gabe's respectful request for his permission. The second had been to see the Admiral, whose approval was gruff but not grudging; "You'll do," he said to Cara after they'd talked for a while, and Gabe had later told her that was the highest praise the man ever gave.

No, the difficult part had been the third visit, one they had put off. But they discovered they'd both decided independently it needed to be done, which made it an obligation they couldn't ignore.

So they'd gone to the quiet, suburban home of Gwen and Earl Waldron, where just months before they'd gone to give them the news they'd expected but dreaded, but also the closure they'd needed. They'd thought about waiting, giving them more time, but Gabe finally said time wasn't going to heal this wound, and they'd gone ahead.

And found, amazingly, that although surprised, Hope's parents welcomed the news.

"It feels right," Gwen said. "You're the two people closest to our little girl, and we know you'll never forget her."

"We never could," Cara had told them gently. And someday, she'd thought, if there was a little girl in their lives, perhaps her name would be Hope.

And now they were back again.

Earl opened the door to Gabe's knock, and stared in surprise. Gwen came up behind him, and her brows rose in a surprise that echoed her husband's.

"Well, now, I figured you two would be busy as bees, today being the day before your wedding. In fact, I was about to call and see if there was anything I could do to help."

"Thank you," Cara said as the pair ushered them inside, "but there's not even much for me to do, except show up."

"Redstone has the wedding thing down pat," Gabe said with a grin. "They've had lots of practice recently, it seems."

"Besides," Cara said, "we wanted to bring you something."

"Us?" Gwen asked.

"It's…well, sort of our wedding present to you."

"Well, that's a twist," Earl said.

Cara glanced at the man who, this time tomorrow, would be her husband. Gabe nodded, and she held out the small book, bound in Hope's vivid purple.

Gwen took it, a puzzled look on her face. Then she saw the title and name on the cover and gasped.

"We thought you should have these," Gabe said. "Hope's personality, her heart, is all over them."

"And know that our own copy will come along wherever we go, so that we will always have Hope with us, too," Cara said.

Hope's parents stared down at the little book of their daughter's stories, including the ones Ryan Barton had been able to recover from the hard drive in Hope's laptop, which had somehow survived with data partially intact. Gwen traced the golden words, *Always Hope*, that gleamed on the cover.

Cara felt her own eyes brim at the raw emotion on those two much-loved faces. And was flooded with gratitude that Gabe had instantly agreed with her idea about this book, and in fact had found the self-publisher himself, through Redstone. Of course.

At that thought, she wondered for a moment how Crystal was doing in her new life; it had taken only a word from Gabe to his boss and an entire new life had opened up for the young woman. She'd hesitated to leave Miriam, but the woman had encouraged her to grab the opportunity; you didn't often get the chance to pick and choose your place in an organization as incredible as Redstone. *The golden touch balanced by the golden rule,* Gabe had told her, the phrase coined in a news magazine about Redstone, was, in fact, true.

She felt Gabe's arm come around her and leaned into him. She remembered when she'd made him read Hope's piece about him, remembered the odd combination of relief and pain that had shown in his face as he did. And how he'd responded when she told him, with every bit of the emotion she was feeling, that what Hope had seen as failings, she found reasons for pride and respect.

And wondered what it was going to be like to be, as Josh had told her she would be, married to Redstone.

Married to Gabriel Taggert, literally the man of her dreams. She couldn't wait to find out.

* * * * *

*Don't miss the next compelling romance
in the* REDSTONE INCORPORATED *miniseries,
coming your way in December 2008
from Justine Davis and Silhouette Romantic Suspense!*

The Colton family is back!
Enjoy a sneak preview of
COLTON'S SECRET SERVICE
by Marie Ferrarella, part of
THE COLTONS: FAMILY FIRST *miniseries.*
Available from Silhouette Romantic Suspense
in September 2008.

He cautioned himself to be leery. He was human and he'd been conned before. But never by anyone nearly so attractive. Never by anyone he'd felt so attracted to.

In her defense, Nick supposed that Georgie could actually be telling him the truth. That she was a victim in all this. He had his people back in California checking her out, to make sure she was who she said she was and had, as she claimed, not even been near a computer but on the road these last few months that the threats had been made.

In the meantime, he was doing his own checking out. Up close and exceedingly personal. So personal he could feel his blood stirring.

It had been a long time since he'd thought of himself as anything other than a law enforcement agent of one type or other. But Georgeann Grady made him remember that beneath the oaths he had taken and his devotion to duty, there beat the heart of a man.

A man who'd been far too long without the touch of a woman.

He watched as the light from the fireplace caressed the outline of Georgie's small, trim, jean-clad body as she moved about the rustic living room that could have easily come off the set of a Hollywood Western. Except that it was genuine.

As genuine as she claimed to be?

Something inside of him hoped so.

He wasn't supposed to be taking sides. His only interest in being here was to guarantee Senator Joe Colton's safety as the latter continued to make his bid for the presidency. Everything else was supposed to be secondary, but, Nick had to silently admit, that was just a wee bit hard to remember right now.

Earlier, before she'd put her precocious handful of a daughter to bed, Georgie had fed his appetite by whipping up some kind of a delicious concoction out of the vegetables she'd pulled from her garden. Vegetables that, by all rights, should have been withered and dried. She'd mentioned that a friend came by on occasion to weed and tend it. Still, it surprised him that somehow she'd managed to make something mouthwatering out of it.

Almost as mouthwatering as she looked to him right at this moment.

Again, he was reminded of the appetite that hadn't been fed, hadn't been satisfied.

And wasn't going to be, Nick sternly told himself. At least not now. Maybe later, when things took on a more definite shape and all the questions in his head were answered to his satisfaction, there would be time to explore this feeling. This woman. But not now.

Damn it.

"Sorry about the lack of light," Georgie said, breaking into his train of thought as she turned around to face him. If she noticed the way he was looking at her, she gave no indication. "But I don't see a point in paying for electricity if I'm not going to be here. Besides, Emmie really enjoys camping out. She likes roughing it."

"And you?" Nick asked, moving closer to her, so close that a whisper would have trouble fitting in. "What do you like?"

The very breath stopped in Georgie's throat as she looked up at him.

"I think you've got a fair shot of guessing that one," she told him softly.

* * * * *

Be sure to look for COLTON'S SECRET SERVICE
and the other following titles from
THE COLTONS: FAMILY FIRST *miniseries:*
RANCHER'S REDEMPTION by Beth Cornelison
THE SHERIFF'S AMNESIAC BRIDE by Linda Conrad
SOLDIER'S SECRET CHILD by Caridad Piñeiro
BABY'S WATCH by Justine Davis
A HERO OF HER OWN by Carla Cassidy

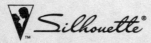

Romantic
SUSPENSE

Sparked by Danger, Fueled by Passion.

The Coltons Are Back!

Marie Ferrarella

Colton's Secret Service

The Coltons: Family First

On a mission to protect a senator, Secret Service agent
Nick Sheffield tracks down a threatening message only
to discover Georgie Gradie Colton, a rodeo-riding single
mom, who insists on her innocence. Nick is instantly
taken with the feisty redhead, but vows not to let his
feelings interfere with his mission. Now he must figure
out if this woman is conning him or if he can trust her
and the passion they share....

Available September wherever books are sold.

Look for upcoming Colton titles
from Silhouette Romantic Suspense:

RANCHER'S REDEMPTION by Beth Cornelison, Available October
THE SHERIFF'S AMNESIAC BRIDE by Linda Conrad, Available November
SOLDIER'S SECRET CHILD by Caridad Piñeiro, Available December
BABY'S WATCH by Justine Davis, Available January 2009
A HERO OF HER OWN by Carla Cassidy, Available February 2009

Visit Silhouette Books at www.eHarlequin.com   SRS27598

REQUEST YOUR FREE BOOKS!

2 FREE NOVELS PLUS 2 FREE GIFTS!

Silhouette® Romantic

SUSPENSE

Sparked by Danger, Fueled by Passion!

YES! Please send me 2 FREE Silhouette® Romantic Suspense novels and my 2 FREE gifts (gifts are worth about $10). After receiving them, if I don't wish to receive any more books, I can return the shipping statement marked "cancel." If I don't cancel, I will receive 4 brand-new novels every month and be billed just $4.24 per book in the U.S. or $4.99 per book in Canada, plus 25¢ shipping and handling per book plus applicable taxes, if any*. That's a savings of at least 15% off the cover price! I understand that accepting the 2 free books and gifts places me under no obligation to buy anything. I can always return a shipment and cancel at any time. Even if I never buy another book from Silhouette, the two free books and gifts are mine to keep forever.

240 SDN EEX6   340 SDN EEYJ

Name	(PLEASE PRINT)	
Address		Apt. #
City	State/Prov.	Zip/Postal Code

Signature (if under 18, a parent or guardian must sign)

Mail to the Silhouette Reader Service:
IN U.S.A.: P.O. Box 1867, Buffalo, NY 14240-1867
IN CANADA: P.O. Box 609, Fort Erie, Ontario L2A 5X3

Not valid to current subscribers of Silhouette Romantic Suspense books.

Want to try two free books from another line?
Call 1-800-873-8635 or visit www.morefreebooks.com.

* Terms and prices subject to change without notice. N.Y. residents add applicable sales tax. Canadian residents will be charged applicable provincial taxes and GST. Offer not valid in Quebec. This offer is limited to one order per household. All orders subject to approval. Credit or debit balances in a customer's account(s) may be offset by any other outstanding balance owed by or to the customer. Please allow 4 to 6 weeks for delivery. Offer available while quantities last.

Your Privacy: Silhouette is committed to protecting your privacy. Our Privacy Policy is available online at www.eHarlequin.com or upon request from the Reader Service. From time to time we make our lists of customers available to reputable third parties who may have a product or service of interest to you. If you would prefer we not share your name and address, please check here. ☐

SRS08R

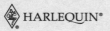
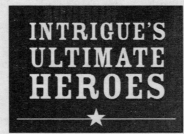

Silhouette®
Romantic
SUSPENSE

COMING NEXT MONTH

#1527 NATURAL-BORN PROTECTOR—Carla Cassidy
Wild West Bodyguards
When Melody Thompson returns to her hometown to investigate her sister's murder, she runs straight into a mysterious and intriguing neighbor, ex-rancher-turned-bodyguard Hank Tyler. The killer comes for Melody, and only Hank can keep her safe—but will their instant attraction put them in even greater danger?

#1528 COLTON'S SECRET SERVICE—Marie Ferrarella
The Coltons: Family First
On a mission to protect a senator, Secret Service agent Nick Sheffield tracks down a threatening message, only to discover Georgie Gradie Colton. The rodeo-riding single mom insists on her innocence. Nick is taken with the feisty redhead, and he must figure out if this woman is conning him or if he can trust her and the passion they share....

#1529 INTIMATE ENEMY—Marilyn Pappano
A secret admirer turned stalker sends lawyer Jamie Munroe into hiding in the least likely of places—the home of ex-lover Russ Calloway. Russ and Jamie have a stormy history, but his code of honor won't let him stand idly by while her life is in danger. Being so close again brings up emotions that may be just as risky....

#1530 MERCENARY'S HONOR—Sharron McClellan
Running for her life in Colombia, reporter Fiona Macmillan needs mercenary Angel Castillo's help. She has an incriminating tape of the Colombian head of national security executing a woman, and the man will kill to get it back. Now Fiona and Angel must learn to trust each other— and resist giving in to passion—to escape with their lives.

SRSCNM0808